RINGS ON WINGS

LOVE IN MOTION

TRACY BROEMMER

Rings on Wings

by

Tracy Broemmer

Sweet Romance

Published by Tracy Broemmer

Edited by Lexie Broemmer

Cover Photo: Deposit Photos

Cover Design: Tracy Broemmer

CHAPTER ONE

JULIE

"Jules? Did you hear me?"

I blink at my friend Dani and finally pull it together enough to nod. I even manage to smile.

"Yeah, Dani!" Of course, I'm excited for Dani and Eric. They're having a baby. It's their first. What's not to be happy about? Dani and I have been friends since kindergarten. *Besties!* I want Dani to have it all—perfect marriage, wonderful husband, and a baby. *A family.* She deserves it.

But for just a half a second there, Dani's news hurts.

Because once upon a time, I thought I was going to have the same thing. Truman Woolff and I were a thing for four years. From the time we were seniors in high school until we graduated from college, Truman and I were inseparable.

And then I got pregnant.

Sure, I was old enough to have sex. Old enough to be responsible for a baby. And I was happy about being pregnant. I read all the books I could find on pregnancy and parenting, and I went back and forth on baby names a hundred times before deciding what to name Ryle.

The only difference between Dani and me is that she and Eric are married.

But when I got pregnant, Truman and I split up.

"I'm so excited for you!" I gush, because that little pin prick of pain has passed, and the six years since then, the six years of me and Ryle make me happy. "When are you due? Do you know what you're having? Have you told anyone?"

Dani chuckles and stretches her legs out on her lounge chair. Eric is in their house getting burgers ready to put on the grill. Ryle is with Truman's parents, so I have the evening to myself. Funny how I always think I need a night to myself, but the second I leave Ryle with Truman or anyone in his family, I miss him.

I sip a canned margarita and close my eyes as I put it back down.

"We haven't told anyone yet but our parents," Dani tells me. "And I don't know what it is."

"I love it," I say, eyes still closed. Now that the little wave of envy is gone, I'm excited to think of all the things my best friend is going to experience. Excited that I'll get to share in most of those things, because odds are, Ryle will be my only child.

"Eric's hoping for twins."

"You should definitely punish him for that." I turn my head on my lounge chair and peek at Dani. She grins. One baby is so much more work than I ever imagined. Then again, Dani has Eric, so things will be somewhat easier for her.

"Hey!" Dani lifts her foot and swings it my way to nudge my leg. She misses, but she has my attention, because I'm laughing at her now. "What did you think of Eric's cousin?"

"He was nice." I shrug and rest my eyes again.

"I think we're going to ask him to be the baby's godfather."

"Oh!" I blink and nod, excited all over again. "Yeah, Jerad seemed like a nice guy."

"And we would like you to be the baby's godmother."

I roll my eyes up to see Eric as he rounds our chairs on the way to the grill, a plate loaded with burgers in hand. He's watching me for my reaction to his announcement.

"Really?" I'm too keyed up now to sit still, so I lean forward and when that's not close enough to Dani, I scooch some on my chair.

"Mm-hmm." Dani nods.

"I'm honored, Dani," I say sincerely. She has two sisters and five brothers; I assumed she would choose someone in her family to be the godmother to her baby. "I would love to stand for the baby."

"Good." She nods, and then Eric repeats her, his voice loud and firm.

Now that it's decided, I flop backwards again in the chair and take another drink.

"So." She clears her throat, which is my first indication that she's up to something. Dani sucks at Poker. She could never win Old Maid when we were kids. And she was terrible when we played Clue. She can't bluster or fib; she gets all nervous. Same as now, when she's about to suggest something she knows I won't like.

"No."

"Hear me out."

"Nope."

"He's going to be in town this weekend." She ignores me. "And we thought we could all go out. Maybe get pizza or something."

Is she seriously trying to set me up with Eric's cousin Jerad? Because as nice as the guy is, there's no way I'd want to go out with him. He's cute—got a little cowlick on the back of his head, usually covers it with a ball cap. And he's got a sweet smile. Plays the trumpet in some band where he lives. Sings at his church. And he loves my friend like she's his sister.

But he's not Truman.

I know it's not fair, but since getting pregnant with Ryle and losing Truman, I compare every guy I meet to Truman. No one measures up.

I've dated. I've tried to move on. I spent seven months with a guy when Ryle was three. The guy adored Ryle, and after everything, that was the top priority on my list. I could have settled for him. He would have been good to me and Ryle. But he didn't deserve that. So, I broke it off with him before it got too complicated.

I still go out sometimes, most often with groups of friends from the bank where I work. And I do date occasionally, but I've resigned myself to the fact that it's not meant to be. I loved Truman Woolff so deeply, for so long, I don't have it in my heart to love another man.

At least Ryle has a relationship with Truman and his family.

"Jules, I just want you to be happy," Dani whines.

"I know." I turn my head to look at her again. "And I appreciate that. But remember. There're different roads to happiness, Dani. I've got Ryle. No one's ever going to take away my happy when I have Ryle."

"But you could—"

The buzz of my phone stops her. She watches me pick it up from the edge of my chair. Truman's name flashes on my screen. What the heck? He's in Vegas; Ryle's with his parents. Why would he be calling me? If it were about Ryle, it would be one of his parents calling.

I hold my breath as I tap the screen. I've never told Dani that seeing Truman's name flash on my phone screen still gives me butterflies just the same way it always did.

"Hey."

"Jules."

He uses my nickname. I used to love it when he called me Jules, especially when he was kissing me. And then I hated it after we split up. He never quit calling me Jules, so I got used to it. Sort of. Though it still brings to mind things better left in the past.

But right now, he sounds a little panicked.

"What? What's going on?"

"We're at the hospital—"

"What?" I'm out of my chair faster than bikes out of the starting gate in a motocross. "What's going on? Is Ryle okay? What happ—"

"Jules."

I hear Truman take a breath. But his attempt to calm himself only makes my heart pound harder. Dani scrambles off her chair, sensing my rising panic. She gathers my purse and keys as I slide my bare feet into my sandals.

"What's going on?" she says quietly as I take my keys from her. "Let me drive you."

"Jules, it's not Ryle." Truman's voice is firm, but he still sounds worried. *Oh no.* What if it's Anthony or Lillian? What if his dad had a heart attack? What if— "It's Harper."

"Harper?" I yelp. "What happened to Harper?"

Dani's still watching me, but she takes a step back now. I'm not close with Truman's family, but I like them all. I care about them; and the thought of something happening to any of them makes me sick.

But now that I know Ryle is okay, my adrenaline rush has piqued, and I'll crash from the let down soon.

"She had an accident. I just wanted—"

"I'm on my way," I tell him. I lean toward Dani, kiss her cheek, and then throw a quick wave at Eric.

"You sure? You want me to drive you?" Dani whispers.

"I'm okay."

"Let me know," she says with a nod at my phone still pressed to my ear.

"Thanks." I turn and hurry to my car. Even knowing that Ryle's okay, I desperately need to get to the hospital and see for myself. I need to put my arms around my son and hold him.

And I need to make sure Harper's okay.

In a perfect world, she would be my sister-in-law.

CHAPTER TWO

TRUMAN

The waiting room is crawling with people; we're all packed into a corner under the TV. I've never been into celebrity gossip, but tonight, the entertainment news show is getting under my skin. Ryle shifts on my lap. With his head on my shoulder, his breath is warm on my neck. He's been out for a while now, and even knowing it's going to mess up his schedule for Jules later, I let him sleep. The ER waiting room is no place for kids.

Harper's mother-in-law met us here earlier when the ambulance first brought my sister in. She took Harper and Keith's kids home with her. Keith and my mom are with Harper in the exam room, and Dad's out here with me and Twain. It's not that I don't want Ryle around, but I know he's bored and probably scared, and he would be better off with Jules.

That's why I called her.

Even though I hated to do it.

I always feel like Julie watches my parenting like a microbiologist studying cells under a microscope. Like she's always looking for me to do something wrong.

She's not. Not really.

Once upon a time, my therapist helped me work out that it's guilt. I always assume Jules finds fault with me, that she sees the worst in me, because of things I've said and done.

Labeling my feelings of guilt, of inadequacy as Ryle's dad, hasn't helped me overcome them.

I look up when the automatic doors open. Four people have come in since I called Jules, so I don't hold my breath expecting this one to be her. It's not, but the woman who rushes inside is a familiar face. Mabry Aliston searches the room. The worry in her face eases just a touch when she sees my brother.

Twain stands to hug her when she hurries to him. Mabry and Twain have been seeing each other for a few months now, but to see them together, you might think they've been married for years. They fit together perfectly.

I'm happy for Twain. I like Mabry. She's fun; she's good for my brother.

But seeing Twain eat up the comfort of a loving woman makes me feel green. I had that once. And I was stupid enough to let it go.

"Any word?" Mabry asks as she pulls back from Twain. She glances at me and then Dad.

"Um. She's got some broken ribs. Broken leg." Twain shrugs, but he's quiet. You can read the tension in his face, around his eyes. Harper is the oldest of us; she's bossy and sometimes snippy, but she's also generous and compassionate, and even though she's technically out of danger, Twain and I are still rattled over the reminder that our sister is mortal. We could have lost her.

"What happened?" Mabry leans over to hug my dad.

If Twain and I are rattled, Dad is shell-shocked. Harper's always been Daddy's girl. Dad hugs Mabry back from his spot in the chair.

"Do you want me to take Ryle?" Mabry turns to me. "I can take him home with me."

"Thanks." I shake my head. "Jules is on her way."

"Okay." Mabry nods and looks around like she's taking stock. "Do you guys need anything?"

"Some kid was texting and driving. She t-boned her," Twain says out of nowhere.

Mabry flinches. "Anthony. Are you hungry? Do you want coffee?"

"I'm fine, Mabry," Dad mumbles. "Thanks."

Women are the caretakers. Even Harper. She's hard-as-nails, independent, and holds her own in a board room, but if she were out here and one of us were in the exam room with fractures and cuts and bruises, she would be asking if we need something. Offering to take the kids somewhere. Watching the nurse's desk and the ER doors, waiting for news, for updates.

"Thank God the kids weren't with her." Twain sucks in a big harsh breath and drops back to his seat. Mabry looks at the empty chair beside him and then glances at the woman in the chair next to it. That woman looks like death—pale and sweating like a fever just broke. Mabry perches carefully on the edge of the empty chair and turns toward us.

"Where are they?" Mabry asks Twain.

"Keith's with Harper," I tell her. "Keith's mom has the kids."

"Okay." She nods.

"If she didn't have the broken leg, she'd have been out of her car and ripping that kid to shreds for texting and driving."

I'm exhausted, and I'm hot. Ryle is sticking to me. His hair is sweaty, and his breath is sour. But the constant rise and fall of his chest against mine is the most precious thing in the room. In my life.

Harper has some injuries, and she's going to be inconvenienced with a cast and crutches, but she's going to be okay.

The low laugh that rumbles up from my gut and spills out surprises all of us, most of all me.

"Yeah, she would've," I agree with Twain. "I can see her grabbing the kid by the ear and draggin' her butt outta the car to give her a piece of her mind."

"That's Harper." Twain nods.

The automatic doors open again. Jules rushes in and comes straight toward me, like she spotted me through the glass as she crossed the parking lot. Her dark hair is pinned up in the messy twist that used to drive me wild. I loved pulling her barrette or hair tie through her soft curls and watching them fall over her shoulders when we were younger.

Afraid, as always, that I'll do something stupid, I press my left hand tight to Ryle's back and smooth my right hand over my leg.

"Hey." Jules reaches for Ryle.

I know it's not that she doesn't trust me. There was a time when I took her every action, every time she looked at Ryle when she picked him up after he was with me, as criticism. Like she was checking to find something I did or didn't do. But I've learned from my own parenting of our son that it's just what parents do. When you're apart from your child, you're missing part of yourself, and when you get that part back, you run your fingers over it, and you study it, and then you hold it close for a moment to mend the pieces back together.

We've perfected this part—the sharing, the transferring. She takes a small step back as I stand and hand our son over to her. Ryle's getting too big for her to hold. She's petite, and Ryle's growing up. But she carries him now and then. She wants to hold him now. I get it. My phone call scared her, though it wasn't my intention.

"Mommy?" Ryle blinks, but his eyes close again as he snuggles into her.

"It's Mommy," she whispers and rubs her hand over his back. "How's Harper?"

My family loves Jules. I've never shared anything with them about why we split up, and I don't plan to. Just as I never tell them I wish things were different. That I wish Julie wasn't just the mother of my child, but also my love, my wife.

Julie always got along well with them, but when we split up, she backed away from all of us. I don't blame her, though I miss her. Just as part of the Woolff family dynamic, I miss her.

"She's got some broken bones," I answer. I clear my throat, my voice gruff. I hate that Twain and Mabry and Dad are all watching this awkward interaction.

Then again, maybe they're all in their own little world.

"Oh no." Jules flinches. "What happened?"

"She got t-boned."

"But she'll be okay?" Jules tips her head. Her big brown eyes roam over my face, and for a second, I remember that she used to look at me that way before pressing into me for a hug.

"Yeah." I nod and step away from her.

I've dated. A lot. I'm on the go all the time. I've been out on the town with women—some friends, some girlfriends—in Vegas and Miami and San Diego. I've moved on, but when I'm standing this close to Jules, I don't know how I've been without her for so long.

I do know she'll never forgive me, so there's no point in dwelling on the past.

"Good." She nods and then looks at my dad. "Hey, Anthony. Are you doing okay?"

Dad offers her a small smile and nods.

Jules glances at Mabry and Twain. She and Mabry share a smile, and then my ex ruffles my brother's hair and turns back to me. My gut is mid flip-flop over that gesture when our eyes meet. How does he rate an affectionate touch and me nothing? Twain has Mabry. Harper has Keith. And Mom and Dad have leaned on each other forever. What if I need someone to be with me?

"Call me," Jules tells me. "If you need something."

I nod and watch her walk away with our son still asleep in her arms.

I should follow her. Offer to carry Ryle to her car.

But she's made it clear that nothing I do for her and Ryle will make up for the past.

CHAPTER THREE

JULIE

As much as I don't want to bump into Truman, when Ryle tells me the next day he wants to see Harper, I can't say no. Harper and Keith babysit Ryle sometimes, and Ryle and their son Ethan are thick as thieves. Besides, I'm worried about Harper, too. I know Truman told me she'll be okay, but I still want to see for myself.

It's Saturday, I tell myself as Ryle climbs into the car. Truman will be busy doing something, so I won't see him. He's into real estate, following in Anthony's footsteps, although Anthony does a better job balancing work and family. Maybe Truman left for Vegas today. I still don't know why he was here last night and not in Vegas. I didn't want to ask questions last night at the hospital.

Once Ryle is settled in his booster seat, he buckles his seat belt, and then beams up at me.

"Good job!" I hold my fist out and wait for him to knuckle me. Not sure who taught him that, but it's his thing now.

His sweet smile morphs into an ornery grin. I shut the door and hurry around the car to get in. "Now, Ryle, you have to remember Aunt Harper is gonna be in pain. She might be sleeping. She might be grouchy. You need—"

"Ethan says Aunt Harper is always grouchy."

I peek at my son in the rearview mirror, amused that he and Ethan discuss Harper. I'm sure they discuss me, too, and I'm sure Ryle says I'm grouchy, too.

"Well, just remember, she's going to have a cast on her leg. And she won't be able to get up and move around easily. Okay?"

"Yep." He's looking out the window, but Ryle nods when he answers me.

Dani called me last night when I got home to check on Harper. They don't know each other that well, but Dani does know Truman's family. Dani doesn't know the real reason we split up, either. I just can't bring myself to talk about it, and I'm not sure if it's because it makes me feel bad or because I'm still trying to protect Truman.

The drive to Harper and Keith's house takes all of seven minutes. Ryle scrambles out of the car before I even have my door open. I start to call after him again to remind him Harper might be sleeping, but he runs up the circle drive and opens the front door, leaving me behind. I flinch as the door closes behind him, but then again, Ryle's a good boy. He might get wound up sometimes, but he doesn't get too loud on a normal day. I can't imagine he would do something to upset Harper now.

It's summertime in Basset, and it's sticky. Late morning sun bakes the cobbled driveway and burns the back of my neck as I make my way to the porch. Wondering who's here, I catch myself before I knock and look over my shoulder, this time paying attention to the cars in the drive rather than the temperature. Lillian's Cooper is here, but that doesn't surprise me. Doesn't bother me, either. Sometimes the way she looks at me makes me feel bad, like I'm cold and unforgiving, but she's never rude to me.

And I suppose I have been unforgiving.

I take a quick breath and steel myself to see Truman's mom and sister and then knock on the door. The house is one of those monster mansions in a gated community—complete with its own golf club. Harper's got the same drive and business acumen that Truman does, but somehow she handles family and work better than Truman, too. She has someone clean her house every other week, but I don't fault her for that. It frees her up to be with her kids when she's not working.

"Julie!" Lillian wears a genuine smile when she opens the door to me. "We wondered if you were coming or if Ryle tooled over here on his battery-powered Jeep."

"Shh!" I laugh and shake my head. "If he hears you, he'll want to do that next time."

"C'min." Lillian reaches for me, but when I do step inside, she drops her hand. I hear Ryle and Ethan's voices coming from down the hall. They must be in the kitchen. Probably angling for cookies. I hope they're not bothering Harper.

"How's Harper?" I keep my voice down in case she's trying to rest. She could be in the family room, right next to the foyer here, or she could be in the den or the kitchen or even out back. I'm fairly certain she's not upstairs in the master bedroom, and if she's anything like me, not being able to sleep in her own bed will only make her grouchier. But unless they've installed an elevator that I know nothing about, I doubt Harper can make it to the second floor right now.

"She's a little doped up," Lillian says honestly. "But she's rest—"

"She's right here!" Harper calls from the family room. "And bored out of her mind."

Lillian raises her eyebrows at me, and we share another laugh. She leads me into the family room where Harper's propped on the couch with a couple of pillows. Another pillow is plumped up under a purple cast that covers her right foot, ankle, and calf.

"Hey." I cringe when I see the bruises and cuts on Harper's face. "How are you feeling?"

"Not gonna lie," Harper says with a goofy smile. "At the moment, I feel beat up and black and blue and a little bit high."

She probably is a little bit high. I laugh softly and put my keys and purse on the coffee table in front of the sofa.

"Twain said broken ribs, too?"

"Turns out, no." She rests her head on the pillows at her back and closes her eyes. "Just very bruised and sore."

"Well, that's good, right?"

"Good is relative," Harper mumbles.

"Ryle wanted to check on you," I tell her as I perch on a wing back chair that sits at an angle to the sofa. "Although, now it seems like he played me for a play date with Ethan."

Harper snorts and squints at me through narrowed eyes. "He came in to talk to me for a minute."

"Yeah?"

"He did," she promises. "Even gave me a kiss."

Her promise makes me feel better about the fact that my son is now in her kitchen, probably making a mess with some kind of snack. But now, sitting here with Harper and Lillian I don't know what to say.

"The other driver broke her wrist," Harper tells me. Before I can respond, she shows me another goofy, lopsided grin, "I hope that means she can't text for a while."

"I assume she got the ticket?"

"She did."

A cell phone rings, but I don't move. I know it's not mine. Harper flinches, so I figure it must be hers. Lillian springs out of the recliner and hurries to the sofa. She practically has to pat Harper down to find her phone.

"Thanks, Mom," Harper mumbles. "I feel like I just went through security at the airport."

The mention of the airport makes me wonder about Truman, why he was in town last night when he was supposed to have flown to Vegas yesterday.

Lillian swats Harper on the arm and rolls her eyes when Harper yelps dramatically.

"Hello?"

Harper looks at me when Lillian turns and walks out of the room.

"Thanks for coming to see me," she says quietly. "Mom's great, but she just keeps telling me to go to sleep."

"She's a mom," I answer, but Harper and I share a smile. "Does it hurt much?"

"Mmm." She shrugs and nods. "Yeah, when the pain meds wear off. Like now."

"Want me to get you a pill?"

"Nope." She sighs and closes her eyes for a minute. "I don't want to get hooked on them. Maybe just some Tylenol?"

"Sure." I'm on my feet before I realize I don't know where she keeps anything. I've been here often enough through the years to drop Ryle off or pick him up, but I've never been in this house as a guest. She and Keith moved in after Truman and I split up.

"Kitchen cabinet to the right of the sink."

"Got it. Be right back."

The house is beautiful. I notice framed family photos as I head down the hall. Harper and Keith have three kids— Ethan, Hattie, and Craig. They're smart kids, just like their mother and their uncles. I don't see as much of Hattie and Craig as I do Ethan.

The hall opens into a big, bright kitchen with white cabinets, stainless steel appliances, and slate gray counter tops. A deep green vase in the center of the table adds a splash of color, the fresh flower arrangement an explosion of pastels. Ethan and Ryle's voices are on the go now; I hear the door close and know they went out back.

As I make way to the cabinet to get Harper's Tylenol, I look around to make sure Ryle didn't help leave a mess anywhere. But I don't see anything other than a plastic cup in the sink. Relieved, even though I know my son is well-behaved, I grab the Tylenol and then stop, wondering if Harper has something to drink.

Just in case, I decide to take her some water. I check another cabinet and find bright green Fiestaware dishes. On the shelf above the place settings, I see water glasses, so I take one down and fill it with ice and water. Her refrigerator is covered in pictures, and I freeze when I see one of Ryle and Truman. It's jolting to see a picture of my son, here in her house—one that I've never seen before. Truman has my son slung over his shoulder in a fireman's carry. From the look on Ryle's face, he's eating it up.

I scan the rest of the pictures, and a hollow pit forms in my stomach. There are several of Ryle—with Truman, with Truman's parents, his sister and brother. In every picture, both Truman and Ryle look happy. While I love seeing the proof that Truman loves our son, it breaks my heart, too. Once upon a time, I wanted to be part of this family.

But Truman didn't want anything to do with it.

And now, I see proof that he and my son are family. And I'm not part of it.

I turn away from the fridge, feeling like a voyeur, like I've seen something that wasn't intended for me, and take the Tylenol and water to Harper. Lillian is still gone; Harper has her eyes closed. I stand for a moment and eye her bruises, feeling again like an outsider.

"Hey." She clears her throat when she opens her eyes and sees me standing there again. "Thank you."

"Of course."

"Would you do me a favor?" she asks and then she grins sheepishly. "Another one."

"Sure." I nod and hand her the two pills. She throws them back easily and then takes the glass of water. I watch her drink, my eyes caught on a cut in her upper lip.

"Will you let Ryle stay and play?"

"I don't want to wear you out," I argue.

"Mom's here. Ryle keeps Ethan busy."

I swallow any further argument. I don't want it to look like I brought Ryle over to dump him on her. But then, if I were in her position, it would help to have Ethan over to keep Ryle busy.

"Do you promise to call me if he gets in the way?"

"Ryle's never in the way—"

"Harper—"

"Yes." She nods and squeezes her eyes closed. "Yes, I promise."

CHAPTER FOUR

Truman

I'm distracted when I park my BMW in the circle drive in front of my sister's house. The voice on the other end of the phone is filling me in on the details about the latest club I'm looking at in Vegas. This one isn't on the strip. In fact, it's old and outdated, and I'm trying to decide if I want to invest or walk away. I was supposed to fly there yesterday to meet with the owners, but I cancelled the trip at the last minute.

It's summertime, and I want to spend more time with Ryle. Actually, it was last winter when I realized I wasn't necessarily getting bored on my job. But where the traveling used to be fun, exciting, it just doesn't appeal to me as much these days. It has everything and nothing at all to do with Julie, but even more so with Ryle.

My son is growing up, and I'm missing it. I was in Reno when Julie did the pregnancy test. What's a guy in his early twenties want with a baby? I was living the dream—traveling first class all over the states, eating in the best, trendiest places, and making more money than I knew what to do with. More money than I needed, considering my parents are real estate tycoons and I was brought up in money.

"Okay, thanks Jack." I end the call and rub my eyes. I'm exhausted. They let Harper go home last night, but it was late when we left the hospital. I could have gone on home, but since Jules had come to pick up Ryle, I didn't have any immediate need to leave. And the rest of my family was in the waiting room, so I stayed. Twain and I traded insults for a while until Dad shut us up. We watched hours of mindless TV. And Mabry and I walked down the block to a fast-food taco joint when we got hungry. Twain stayed back with Dad.

But even when I got home at midnight, I couldn't sleep. I was keyed up about Harper, but I also just felt off. I'd spent the evening with my family, and then I had to break away and be by myself. Twain and Mabry aren't living together yet, but they left the hospital hand in hand, and that only drove home the fact that I was alone.

With a yawn, I grab my keys and phone and climb out of the driver's seat. And that's when I realize I'm parked behind Julie's car. What's she doing here? I stand for a moment and stare at it, like it might give up some answers. Why is she here? Would she ever forgive me? If she did, could she love me again? I'm standing in the drive, staring at her car like it's a Magic 8 ball—like maybe if I pick it up and shake it, I'll figure something out.

Well, no, the car's not going to give me answers, and a Magic 8 Ball would probably tell me to concentrate and ask again. Whereas a look at Julie tells me no, period. She's coming down the drive as I walk up toward the house. She slows when she sees me, but she keeps walking.

"Hey."

Usually, we can speak to each other like adults. No matter the things said between us back then, we decided when Ryle was born that we would be friendly. Today, though, I stare at her blankly, my social skills apparently on hiatus.

"Ryle wanted to see Harper," she tells me.

"Is he still here?"

Jules bits her lip and nods. "Yeah. Harper asked if I would let him stay and play with Ethan for a while."

"Okay." I nod and shift my weight on my feet. Jules is wearing cut off denim and a loose-fitting sleeveless blouse. No makeup. No jewelry. She's never been prettier. She eyes my golf shorts and then meets my eyes.

"Playing today?"

"No." I tuck my hands in my pockets and rock up on my toes, uncomfortable with how things are between us but in the dark about how to fix anything. "Just thought I'd see how Harper is."

Jules stares at me silently for a moment, and I get the feeling she wants to say something else. But she doesn't. She simply nods and moves past me on the drive.

"I could..." I turn to watch her and shrug awkwardly when she looks at me expectantly "I could bring Ryle home later."

"Sure." She nods and takes another step away from me. "Or, if you're too busy, just have Harper call me."

I wish I had a comeback for that. But I don't. I watch her watch me as she walks backwards to her car, and then she turns her back to me, rounds the car, and gets in. She drives off without waving or even looking back. I watch her until she's out of sight, and then I look up at the sky and around at Harper and Keith's property. The place is beautiful.

But maybe the best thing about their house, their lives, is their kids, their family life.

At least I'll get to see Ryle, I remind myself as I turn and continue to the porch. I tap on the door and let myself in just as Mom is about to pull it open. She smiles at me and puts her finger on her lips. Harper must be sleeping. I almost laugh at the argument that probably went on between the two of them before Harper crashed.

Harper thinks napping is a weakness. She rarely sleeps more than five hours a night. And she insists she'll sleep when she's dead. Until then, she's got far too much to do to lounge.

"The boys are out back," Mom whispers to me. I nod and hurry through the house only to go out the back door. Ethan and Ryle are head-to-head in the grass, bent over something.

"What're you doing?" I holler.

"Daddy!" Ryle jumps to his feet and runs to me. How did I ever think boardrooms and mergers were better than this? I scoop him up and continue on to high five Ethan.

"An anthill?" I lean over to see better, but yes, it appears my son and nephew are observing an anthill.

"My dad said red ants hurt you."

"Are those red ants?" I ask quickly.

"No." Ethan shrugs and shakes his head, apparently disappointed.

"Let's play whiffle ball." It seems like a good idea to distract them, and it sounds like fun.

"Yes!" Ethan and Ryle both holler. I put Ryle down and watch the two of them run to the garage to get the ball and bat.

"What's going on, Uncle Truman?"

My nephew Craig moseys out the back door of the house and crosses the lawn to stand by me.

"Epic whiffle ball game," I tell him. "Is Hattie home?"

"She's in her room."

"Well, go get her. We're talking high stakes game here."

"What does that mean?"

"It means," I tell him as Ryle and Ethan charge back out with three bats—only one of them is an actual plastic bat—and a bucket of balls, "Losers buy the winners ice cream."

"I don't have any money," Craig tells me.

"Then I guess you'd better win."

CHAPTER FIVE

Julie

I'm fixing dinner when the door opens, and Ryle explodes into the kitchen.

"Mom!" He throws himself at me and loops his arms around my legs. I look down at him and then at the door when I hear it close. Truman stands there with a small smile on his face. He's still wearing the golf shorts and shirt he had on earlier, but he doesn't look as crisp as he did then. In fact, his face is flushed and his hairline is sweaty, like he's been working out.

"Hey." I turn my attention to my son and remind myself I have no business looking at Truman so closely. So what if we made this child together? We broke up a long time ago, and wishing things were different doesn't work.

"We played whiffle ball!" Ryle throws his arms out like he's trying to rile up a crowd in a stadium. "And we won!"

"Dude!" I stick my hand out for a high five and peek at Truman while Ryle slaps my palm. "Way to go!"

"Dad says I'm a natural," he continues. "He says I have an arm like a Baby Ruth."

I bite my lips to hold back the laugh and cut my eyes to Truman again.

"Babe Ruth, huh?" I tip my head and narrow my eyes at Ryle. "Why have I never seen this Babe Ruth arm?"

Ryle stares at me with wide eyes. "You should have played with us, Mom!"

"Guess so," I agree. "Go wash your hands."

Ryle scampers out of the kitchen to wash his hands. I glance at Truman again and go back to finishing dinner. Ryle loves chicken, so I have some in the oven. I check the spaghetti noodles, decide they're done, and carry the pot over to the sink to drain them.

"Chicken parm, huh?" Truman asks. His voice is still far away, but I feel his eyes on me. The pot slips, and I splash a bit of the boiling water on my hand. I gasp and pull it away quickly, but before I can say anything, Truman's there, standing beside me. "Did you burn yourself?"

I nod and insist that I'm fine. It burns, but it wasn't that big of a deal.

Still, Truman takes my hand in his and eyes my red skin carefully.

"Run cold water on it," he tells me. "I'll do this."

Like I'm a little kid, he flips on the faucet and then takes the pot from me to finish draining the noodles.

"Does he still eat it without sauce?"

I laugh softly and nod when Truman looks at me. Ryle loves breaded chicken strips covered in melted mozzarella, served with plain spaghetti noodles.

"I have a confession to make," Truman says quietly.

"What?" I watch him suspiciously as he carries the pot of noodles back to the stove. What could he possibly have to confess to me? Nothing he does is any of my business now, nothing other than stuff about Ryle. I trust him, though. Even with how rough things were when I first got pregnant, I trust Truman with our son.

"We had ice cream."

Ice cream.

I snort when Truman looks at me. Now he looks like a kid, like Ryle, the way his chin is tucked and he's looking at me through his thick lashes, like he knows he's in trouble.

"Mom!" Ryle trots back into the kitchen. "Grandma hit a home run!"

I turn the water off and dab at the burn spot with a dish towel. Sounds like a fun ball game. I swallow the little bitter taste in my mouth. I should have stayed. Then again, if I had, they wouldn't have played, or I wouldn't have played, and the afternoon wouldn't have been as fun for Ryle.

"Grandma played?" I ask Ryle and then look at Truman for confirmation.

"Yeah!" Ryle drags his chair out from under the table and climbs into it. I catch myself before directing him to get the silverware out. He can't reach the plates and cups, so his job is silverware and napkins. But with Truman here, with Ryle so excited about his afternoon with Truman, I decide maybe rules and jobs don't matter.

Especially if Ryle's already had ice cream.

Truman steps around me, leaning in to look over my shoulder at my hand.

"It's fine," I mumble and drop my hands to my sides. It's a little sore, but I don't want to make a big deal over nothing. I twist around and watch as Truman sets the table. For two. Ryle watches him place the silverware just so and then looks at Truman with a frown.

Now my heart hurts much worse than my hand.

Truman never stays for dinner when he brings Ryle home. He usually walks him to the door, says hi to me, goodbye to Ryle, and then heads back to his car.

Tonight, something about the two place settings at the table and the three of us in the room together feels wrong. And what makes it worse is that Ryle notices.

"Daddy, eat with us," he directs his comment to Truman, but he looks at me when he says it. Ryle's never asked why Truman and I don't live together, why we're not a family like Ethan's mom and dad or other kids he's around. But surely, he wonders. He's six; he went to kindergarten. He's been exposed to all sorts of family dynamics now, and while I'm sure he's not the only kid in his class whose parents aren't together, he has to wonder why his family isn't.

Truman cuts his eyes to me silently. Ryle's still looking at me, so Truman shakes his head and puts his hands up to me, palms out. Is he just being the good guy? Trying to slip out so I'm not uncomfortable with him being here? Or does he have other plans?

I know Truman's dated. A lot. I know he's been seriously involved a time or two since we broke up. What I don't know is why neither of those relationships lasted. It's not my business, but I'll admit I do wonder about it now and then.

"Can Daddy eat with us, Mom?" Ryle breaks the awkward silence.

"Of course," I say just as Truman says, "Daddy's gotta go, Ryle."

Ryle slumps in his chair and picks up his fork. He stares at it silently, the light in his eyes dimmed now. Truman and I stare at each other for a moment, and then I remember Truman's a big shot with big money, and he probably has a hot date with a smokin' hot blonde. Or a fiery redhead.

Or anyone who's not me.

I turn away to get the chicken from the oven.

"Up to you, Truman." I hope I sound nonchalant. I throw in a shrug as I put the cookie sheet with the chicken on the stovetop. "There's plenty here if you want to stay."

"Stay, Daddy!" Ryle sounds so hopeful, I hold my breath. This is why I never wanted Truman to come inside. It's one thing that he's moved on from us, but I hate to see our son disappointed.

"I can't barge in on you guys, bud," Truman says apologetically. "This is your mom's time with you. We had a good day, though, didn't we?"

"Truman." I turn and grab a plate from the table, eyeing him as I do. "You're welcome to stay and eat dinner with us."

Ryle cheers again, and the chair bangs around and screeches on the floor. When I look over my shoulder, I see him climbing up to sit on his knees. He stares at Truman, his hands folded as if in prayer. Wonder where he learned that.

"Are you sure?" Truman asks me.

"I mean, I have all this sauce, and Ryle's not going to share it with me."

Truman laughs softly, glances at Ryle, and gives in with a small nod.

"Yes!" Ryle throws his fist in the air in celebration. He's not usually so boisterous. It makes me happy—obviously, he had fun today. I'm guessing he's imitating his older cousin Craig with the theatrics.

I like it.

Unfortunately, I like the feeling of sitting down at our little kitchen table with Truman. I'm sure it won't happen again, and I'm sure that Ryle thinks it will. I can handle the disappointment, but I'm not sure Ryle can.

CHAPTER SIX

JULIE

It doesn't take long to tidy up the kitchen, so I end up in the living room with Ryle and Truman. I don't want to disturb them—they're spread out on the floor playing a board game that involves matching—so I slip into the room quietly, grab a spot on the sofa, and pick up the book I've been reading. But as much as I love Kate Carley's books, tonight I'm more interested in my son and his father, and I end up putting the book aside to watch them play.

Ryle has a wicked memory, so I'm not surprised when he beats Truman two times in a row. I can tell Truman's impressed; his eyes get wide every time Ryle makes a match. But he nods and pretends to act exasperated with Ryle, and that makes my son giggle. I rest my head on the sofa and close my eyes, happy to listen to the two of them talking and laughing together.

I let Ryle stay up later than usual. After all, it's summer. And this is a first for him. My only worry is that he might think it's going to happen again. I don't mind that Truman is here, and it wouldn't bother me if Truman was around more often. But it's unusual that he's in town and hanging around here; Truman's a jet-setter. He's always on the go. So, odds are, this isn't going to become a tradition. Not even a semi-normal occurrence.

Which makes me worry that Ryle's going to get hurt.

I wouldn't normally insist that Ryle take a bath before bedtime, but since it is summer and he played whiffle ball, I catch them after their fourth game and send Ryle to the bathroom to get ready for bed. I'm halfway off the sofa when my phone rings.

"I can help him," Truman offers with a nod at the phone. "If you wanna get that."

Ryle didn't hear him, so I could tell Truman to go, and I'll handle it. But I'm feeling pretty mellow, so I decide another half hour with his dad won't hurt.

"Thanks." I nod and drop back to sit in the corner of the sofa. The call is from Dani. I pick it up as Truman disappears from the room.

"Hey."

I laugh softly when I hear Ryle give a loud whoop from down the hall. I wonder if he'd be this excited if it were me hanging around Truman's place. Probably best not to think about that.

"Julie!" Dani sounds out of breath. "How's Harper?"

I talked to Dani last night after I rushed away from her and Eric's house to get to the hospital. But it's natural for her to be concerned and check in again.

"I think she's doing okay," I answer. "I think her biggest issue now is being immobile and drugged for the pain."

Dani chuckles. She knows Harper well enough to know I'm on the money with my observation.

"Ryle wanted to see her, so I took him over there today. She's sore."

"I'm sure she is," Dani agrees. "Did the girl who hit her get a ticket?"

"Yes."

If she wouldn't have, Truman's sister would have hobbled her way into the police station and made a scene about it. Not that I blame her.

"Good." It sounds like Dani's drinking something. "Sorry. Eric and I are eating late."

"No problem." I wonder why she didn't just wait to call me, and I hold my breath, assuming she's about to suggest going somewhere. On a double date.

"So." She clears her throat. I bite my tongue. I'm not remotely interested in going out with Jerad. But I don't want to snap at my best friend, so I can at least wait her out and then say no. "Jerad's in town. Eric and I wondered if you wanna go grab a drink with us. You'll have a designated driver!" Before I can say no, that I'm home with Ryle, Dani continues, "If Truman's parents can't watch Ryle, my sister can."

As much as I like Dani's little sister, I shake my head even as she speaks.

"I can't, Dani," I say hoping I sound disappointed. "Truman's here."

"So, leave Ryle with him. That's perfect!"

Leave it to Dani.

I tuck my chin to my chest and smooth my fingertips over my forehead. Even if I wanted to go out with Jerad, I would feel funny asking Truman to sit around here with Ryle while I was gone.

"No, it's...um." I shrug and look around the room desperately, grasping for something I can say that involves me and Truman needing to talk. "Ryle's been playing some baseball. Truman and I are talking about getting him on Ethan's team. Kind of complicated since the season's already started."

I have no idea if that's true, but it sounds reasonable. And Dani wouldn't have any way of knowing if I'm making it up.

"Oh." She sighs, clearly bummed that I won't join them. "Okay. Ryle's liking baseball, huh?"

"Yeah."

"Told you Eric said he's got a home run swing," Dani reminds me. I do remember her saying that now that she's brought it up. Eric and Ryle play baseball and football in their backyard. He's never told me I have a future quarterback on my hands, but Ryle has impressed him with baseball.

For a second, I feel guilty for not paying attention to that. If Ryle had told me he wanted to play, I would have signed him up immediately. Why didn't I pay more attention? I could have asked my son if he wanted to play baseball with Ethan. Maybe Truman should have signed him up, but then, Truman's not around as much as I am.

"You did say that," I agree with Dani.

"Okay, hope you guys get him on a team!" Dani sounds excited again. "We'll be at every game."

When I hang up, the house is quiet. I sit for a second, a little bit sad about the things my little boy has missed. Signing up for baseball is the least of it. My little boy's never been tucked in by his mommy and daddy on the same night. My little boy's never jumped into bed in the middle of the night with both parents after a bad dream. Ryle's never had chocolate chip pancakes with his mom and dad for breakfast.

Maybe none of that's ever crossed Ryle's mind. Maybe I'm projecting. But when Ryle's only six, and he doesn't ever have much to say, it's hard to know what he's thinking.

"You okay?"

Truman's voice from somewhere behind me startles me. I catch my breath, but I manage to hold my body still.

"Yeah." I stand and turn to look at Truman with a nod.

"Did I just hear you use me being here as an excuse not to go out with someone?"

The tiny grin on his face is priceless, the dimple on his chin precious. I used to kiss that grin and dimple and face, and I have to remind myself again that I don't do that anymore. I *can't* do it anymore.

CHAPTER SEVEN

TRUMAN

"Um." Jules stares at me with wide eyes, all innocence, but her lips twitch as I watch her, and finally, she laughs softly. "Maybe."

"'kay." I nod and shove my hands in my pockets, feeling awkward. I haven't been in Julie's space like this in years. "Ryle's out of the shower and in his pjs."

"Good." She offers me a sweet smile, but she's still a little embarrassed that I caught her using me to get out of a date. She tucks her chin to her chest and slips around me, presumably to tuck Ryle in. "I'll be right back."

When she looks back at me over her shoulder, I shrug and then nod, because if she said that, it seems like maybe she wants me to wait for her and not leave. Ryle decided when he was five that he wanted to take showers rather than baths. I suspect Julie still monitors the showers to make sure he's washing everything and not lounging or playing. I did the same, although mostly I just stood with my butt against the sink and talked to him while he did the work. I could smell the baby shampoo and soap Julie still buys for him, so I know he was washing something.

He did peek out at me with his head covered in suds at one point, so I took that as a good sign.

When Ryle stays at my place, and suddenly, I wish he was at my place more often, we read a story at night. I know Jules reads to him, too, but when Ryle and I read, we act it out. Like, if we're reading *The Very Hungry Caterpillar*, Ryle pretends he's eating everything the caterpillar eats in the story. So, Julie might say my bedtime reading style isn't conducive to sleep.

But it's fun.

I know Ryle will want her to read to him, even if I'm here waiting for her to come back. So I wander around her living room, hands still in my pockets, and get to know my ex-girlfriend again. This time, as a grown woman, the mother of my son and not just my high school and college sweetheart.

Julie's house is small, but it's newer than most on her block. The carpet is nice; the woodwork is pristine—no scratches, no dust. A blue afghan is folded on the end of the sand-colored sofa. A recliner in a darker color of sand sets over by the window. She probably rocked Ryle to sleep in that recliner.

Not for the first time, it hits me what Julie went through on her own when she had Ryle. But something about standing in her home, knowing she's down the hall tucking our little boy into bed in their house, really drives the loneliness home. I imagine it was hard for her when Ryle was little.

She's always been good with him, but it hits me as I wait for her to come back, how much work she's done with and for my son.

I wish things were different.

Moving through the living room, I head back to the kitchen. I won't leave until she comes back, but I feel like I shouldn't be roaming through her house without Ryle. Instead of getting comfortable on her sofa, I pull out a chair and sit at the kitchen table again. The dinner dishes are done and put away. The counter and table are spotless. There's a bottle of chewable vitamins on the counter by the toaster. A cup shaped like a dinosaur next to it.

I swing my gaze to the refrigerator and study Ryle's artwork there. There's a picture of what appears to be a superhero of some sort with a car in his hands. Wonder what that symbolizes. I would know if Jules had an accident or something, wouldn't I? Maybe Ryle drew it after Harper's accident?

Another picture hangs on the freezer side. It's obviously a dog, but it has Ryle's name and the date in the top corner, so I assume it was a school assignment. Around the artwork, Jules has peppered the fridge and freezer doors with snapshots. I can't see them all that clearly from where I'm sitting, but a few are bigger prints, and I can make out Ryle's grin and his eyes. Intrigued, I get up to move closer and study the pictures. Most of them are shots of Ryle, some Ryle with Ethan, and some with one of his friends from school. There're a couple pictures of Jules—one with Ryle and one with her friend Dani, both of them all dolled up with drinks in their hands.

I wonder when that was taken. Jules is radiant—the makeup and fancy hairstyle are both gorgeous, but what makes the picture is the smile on her face. She looks happy. Really, truly happy. And while I love that, while it's all I've ever wanted for her, I feel guilty. It wasn't enough that I hurt her; I left her alone with a baby and changed her mind about wanting a relationship in the future. She wouldn't trust just anyone with Ryle, and I appreciate that. But she's too young to be happy alone. Julie's a successful, independent woman, so she doesn't need a man to complete her. She showed me that.

But she should have someone around to love her. To cherish her. Of course, I wish that someone was me, but knowing that's never going to happen makes me wish she would trust again and find someone to grow old with.

Wow.

I give myself a mental shake. What has gotten into me? First the growing resentment with my job, with the travel, being gone away from Ryle so much. Then the canceling work travel, putting the brakes on a few of my big acquisitions, and handing more responsibility over to my assistant. And now this? Wishing my ex had someone to grow old with?

And I'm not even drinking.

"Hey."

I huff out a sigh and turn when I hear Jules behind me. She eyes me curiously as she moves with hesitation to the table.

"Is he out?"

"Oh yeah." She laughs and raises her eyebrows. "He must have played hard today."

Holding the eye contact, I can only nod.

"I thought." She clears her throat and looks away. "I thought maybe you got tired of waiting on me and left."

"Nah." I shrug and go back to the table to sit. "Just didn't feel right to make myself at home in the living room."

She nods but keeps her eyes averted.

"So, who asked you out?" I ask with a grin. "Anyone I know?"

"Dani's trying to set me up with Eric's cousin."

"Oh."

"He's a nice guy." She shrugs. "But I'm not interested."

"It's okay to find someone, Julie."

I don't mean to say it. The words are out of my mouth before I even know I'm thinking them. She jerks her gaze back to me and meets my eyes.

"I mean, I know…" I hold my breath for a second and then figure why not? Already started, might as well go all in. "I know I hurt you. But there's someone out there who will treat you like a queen and love Ryle like his own."

I don't know what I want her to say, but the longer she stares at me, the more I worry what she's thinking. Finally, she swallows hard, shakes her head, and looks away again.

"Do you think you can get Ryle on a baseball team?"

I do think I could. Ryle would like it. But I want to go back to the way she looked at me and then looked away. Jules threw up a stone wall around her heart and her mind when we split up. I used to know her well enough that we finished each other's sentences, that we didn't even have to talk—we just always knew what the other was thinking. Now I have no idea what she thinks, what she wants in life.

"Yeah." I nod. "I'll talk to Keith. He's missed a few games, but I'm sure at his age and that level, it won't be a big deal."

"Good." She flashes me an uneasy smile. "Thanks."

I bite my tongue before I tell her not to thank me. Ryle's my son, too. Of course I want him to play baseball or whatever it is he's interested in. As much as I would like to sit here and dig into the past and the things that broke us, I'm afraid of what it might do to our truce. We're friendly enough now so that Ryle doesn't have to suffer through tension and heartache. But if I push this now, that would likely change.

The last thing I want is to make her angry and end up making things hard for Ryle.

"I should go." I press my hands on the table, wishing she would argue, ask me to stay longer. When she doesn't, I stand and push the chair in. "Thanks for dinner. It was fun."

"It was," she agrees. She doesn't stand when I walk away from the table, but she does call after me to say goodnight.

It was. A good night. Until it wasn't anymore.

CHAPTER EIGHT

JULIE

Ryle and Ethan talk about baseball all the way to the ball field. I peek at them in the rearview mirror when I'm stopped. They're both adorable in their little baseball pants and red t-shirts. Ethan has his ball cap pulled down so hard his ears stick out. Ryle's, on the other hand, barely sits on his head. He's going to need to tug it down a bit, or he'll lose it running the bases.

Truman called me the day after we talked about Ryle playing to tell me he got him on Ethan's team. Since Harper's still in the big cast and not getting around well, I offered to drive Ethan to the game, though I have to admit, I was worried about running into Truman when I picked him up.

I'm still reeling over what he said to me the other night, especially after we had a fun night together with Ryle. Well, I thought we had a fun night together. Apparently, if

Truman enjoyed himself, it was because he was with Ryle. Not me.

It's not even like he said anything mean. There probably aren't a lot of guys who wish their exes well and sincerely want them to find love and happiness with someone else. But Truman's parting words the other night drove home the point that he doesn't want to be with me. He'd balked when I got pregnant. He's changed his tune about Ryle, thankfully, and he's a great dad. But he obviously doesn't want to be that involved in parenting with me. Like, under-one-roof kind of parenting.

Not that I really believed he would ever change his mind. I guess I did what I was worried Ryle would do. Truman stayed for dinner, and I got my hopes up that it meant something. Ryle handled it better than I did.

When I park, the boys jump out of the backseat and hurry across the grass to the field. I start to holler at Ryle to wait, but he's already out of earshot, and besides, it's probably better for him to be excited and rush in with no hesitation than to wait for his mom to walk him over.

I grab my phone and pocket my keys. There's a game on the field right now—a powder blue team and a green team. The early evening sun is right in my face as I move slowly toward the field. Looking for Ryle, and maybe more importantly, for Ryle's coach, I put my hand up to shield my eyes.

And there he is.

Not the coach. Or Ryle.

Truman.

I watch him for a second, my stomach tied in knots over seeing him again. I'm thrilled that he's here to watch Ryle play, but I don't know why he didn't tell me he would be here. And I feel a little prickly after what he said the other night.

He's talking to a guy, I assume another dad, and then suddenly, Ryle stands in front of them, and Truman gives him his full attention. Fascinated by this new Truman, I mosey over to stand a bit closer, but mostly I'm still hidden behind a group of boys, a small set of bleachers, and a tree. Ryle has his glove on now. It looks huge on his skinny little arm, but the salesgirl told me it was better to get him a real glove, not the cute little ones designed for tee-ball.

Judging from the way Ryle is showing it off to Truman, he likes it, but I hold my breath when Truman takes it to study it. My whole body deflates when he nods his approval and hands it back to Ryle with a grin. Shoulders still drooped in relief, I feel a jab of pain right in the feels when Truman reaches up to tug the bill of Ryle's cap down a bit.

A man in a red shirt like Ryle's and Ethan's calls them all down from the dugout and gathers them in a circle. I watch for a moment while the coach talks to the boys and high fives them and finally decide to make my way to a spot on the bleachers. I go around the other side in hopes that Truman won't notice me. There's a group of moms, I assume, clumped together in the middle of the aluminum bleachers. A few of them notice me and wave. I wave in response, but I sit alone a few feet away. I kind of want a moment to watch my little boy play ball.

I look down at my phone when it buzzes.

Thank you again for driving Ethan.

I'm smiling when I answer Harper.

No problem. It's probably easier for Ryle that he and Ethan came together.

"Hey."

Head still tilted down over my phone, I bite my lip when I hear Truman's voice.

"Hi." I press the button to lock the screen and look up at Truman cautiously.

"He looks like a stud."

How could Ryle not look like a stud? Truman Woolff was a three-sport athlete in school—he played baseball, soccer, and basketball. Ryle takes after his dad in a lot of things. That thought hurts just a little. Ryle will never know that Truman didn't want him when I got pregnant; he will never hear that from me. But that doesn't mean I've forgotten the fights Truman and I had over the pregnancy and the future.

With a nod, I look away from Truman and search out Ryle in the group of boys. The coach has them file onto the field and break into partners. Truman, looking casual and effortlessly handsome, stands in front of me, hands in his pockets.

"You got him a nice glove."

Truman's comment draws my attention back to him.

"The salesgirl assured me if he's going to stick with it, it was better to get one a bit bigger."

Truman nods his agreement. "Absolutely."

My phone buzzes again. I feel Truman watching me as I check it.

"Dani? Or Eric's cousin?"

The reminder of him catching me in that little fib the other night is a little mortifying. He's met Eric's cousin, but only once. Truman's never met any of the guys I've dated, and I don't talk about them or dating, in general, around Ryle. I wish he was asking now who's texting because he's jealous and not just to tease me.

"Harper," I answer simply.

"Oh." He nods, obviously surprised that his sister would text me.

"She asked me to send a picture of Ethan."

Truman twists around to look at the boys on the field. They're lined in pairs, playing pitch and catch. Sort of. The good news is, their opponents, dressed in bright orange, don't appear anymore put together than our boys.

I'm watching Ryle and Ethan throw a ball back and forth. They've managed five throws in a row, and I'm seeing that Ryle does have a good arm. I never played baseball or softball, but I understand it and enjoy watching major league games. And I can see that my son has some talent. What comes of that talent remains to be seen.

Truman clears his throat. When I glance at him, he's watching me.

"Can I sit?" He nods at the bleacher beside me.

"Yeah." I shrug and look back at the boys.

I don't watch him climb up over the bottom two bleachers to sit beside me. But from the corner of my eye, I see the lean muscles in his thighs flex and bunch as he moves. When he's sitting beside me, he leans in close and bumps his upper arm to mine.

"You okay?"

Startled by his question, I turn my face to look at him. His face is so close, I can see the flecks of gold in his eyes and smell spearmint on his breath. The smell brings back a hundred memories at once. Kissing him after classes. Hanging out at his parents' house to watch movies with him. Going out after his games to celebrate—pizzas in high school and beers when we were of age.

Right before we broke up.

"You seem upset about something."

I am, but it's ridiculous to be upset about it, so I laugh it off and shake my head. Nothing will come of that stroll down memory lane, so it's best not to go there. And it's silly for me to be upset with him for wishing me well the other night. He wants the mother of his son to be happy. I'm the one being immature, pouting because I read too much into one night at the house.

"I'm good."

CHAPTER NINE

TRUMAN

I want to call her out on that, saying she's good, because to me something feels off. But I remind myself Jules has a life outside of me. No, actually, Julie's life has nothing to do with me now. We're coparenting Ryle, but nothing else about her is any of my business. Including whether or not she's okay right at this minute.

So, rather than poke at her again and make her talk, I nod and turn my attention back to the field. The coaches are calling the boys back to the dugouts now. The umpires—I'm happy to see they look more like dads than young high school kids who wouldn't give the boys enough patience and instruction—are standing at home plate, ready to get the game started.

Ryle's team is taking the field first. Ethan is at first base, and Ryle seems to be playing the other side of the infield. Along with about four other boys. So, either they have two third basemen and two shortstops, or the outfielders are on the infield, too. Not that it matters in tee-ball. I played, and yes, I still remember what it was like. Once that ball is in play, it'll look like a soccer game—all of the boys on the field will follow the ball, rather than covering the appropriate base.

Then again, tee-ball isn't cutthroat. Not like the whiffle ball game we played the other day.

Jules takes a picture of Ethan on first when the first batter steps into the box. Knees bent and glove down, he looks ready for anything. I peek at Ryle, tickled to see him in the same stance, only he's in the middle of four kids playing the left side of the infield.

"So." Jules stretches her legs out making me speechless for a moment or two. I know for a fact her golden brown skin is smooth and soft. She's wearing basic white Cons and no-show socks. I tell myself not to do it, but my eyes trek all the way up her legs to her denim shorts and white t-shirt.

She's everything.

And I let her go. Not true. I pushed her away.

"What's with you being in town so much lately?"

Eyes back on the boys in the field, I hope she doesn't see me flinch. Is she upset that I've been around more?

"I want to be here," I say with a shrug.

When I feel her eyes on me, I flick my gaze to hers. She stares at me boldly, and that ugly scene from years ago crams itself in between us.

"I'm missing out on too much," I mumble. "I'm tired of the traveling."

"Missing out on what?"

"Ryle."

She's quiet for a moment. Finally, she nods and drags her gaze away from me. I sag a little with relief, not that she's the type to say I told you so. But I deserve it.

"Is it okay?"

"Is what okay?" she asks without looking at me.

"If I'm around more."

"Truman." She bumps my arm with hers, but she won't look at me. "Of course it is! Ryle loves spending time with you."

We stop talking, concentrating more on the game, such as it is. Ethan has a pretty good glove; he's caught several balls lobbed and thrown to him. I wonder if the coach put him on first for that reason, or if the boys just picked their spots.

When they're up to bat, I see Ryle peeking at me from the dugout. Knowing it wouldn't be cool to wave at him—if other boys are watching—I give him a nod and the peace sign. He grins and turns away. Ethan is batting. My nephew tags the ball on the first swing and knocks it through a hole on the right side of the infield. The orange team goes after the ball en masse, and Ethan ends up on second base. I glance at Jules; she holds her hand up for a high five, but she's recording Ethan's at bat for Harper.

The high five is the first time we've touched in a long time. Her hand is warm and soft, and for a moment, I remember how we used to walk to classes together, hand in hand.

Ryle takes a few swings to make contact, but when he does, he pops the ball up. It drops around second base, and Ethan and a boy who batted between them move up a base. When Ryle's on first, he looks at me and Jules again. Julie gives him a thumbs up, and I realize she's being a cool mom. No waving to your little boy when he's playing with his buddies.

The game takes right at an hour. They don't do three outs—everyone bats through each inning. They don't keep score; they're all winners. Part of me gets that, but the competitive part of me doesn't like it. On the other hand, both teams come off the field cheering and giggling and acting like happy little boys, and that's what matters.

Ryle and Ethan find us on the bleachers when the game is over. They've both got a juice box in hand and a bag of carrot sticks. The carrot sticks make me cringe; I hope when it's our turn to bring a snack, Julie doesn't go all healthy mom on Ryle.

Both boys are dirty from sliding and diving. Ryle wears his glove on his hand, and it's almost comical how big it is and how little it makes him look. Ethan, on the other hand, has clearly learned things from his cool older brother, Craig. His glove is on top of his hat, still pushed down so far, his ears stick out.

"Dude." Ethan grins. "That was so cool."

Julie and I exchange a look.

"I'm hungry, Mom."

"Eat your carrot sticks," Julie tells Ryle. Her words are like a knife in my heart. She's going to bring blueberries or celery for snack when it's our turn. I just know it.

To my surprise, Ryle tugs his glove off and hands it to Julie, and then grabs a carrot to crunch.

"I can take Ethan home," I offer.

"Are you sure?"

I realize it's not a big deal for her to drive Ethan home, but I don't have any idea how Julie feels about being around Harper. Or the rest of my family, for that matter.

"Yeah." I hold my fist up to Ethan and grin when he knuckles me. "And Keith will be back in town for their next game."

Julie looks at me curiously and finally nods. "Okay."

Instead of watching her climb down the two bleachers to stand, I purposely look away. No need to be moony eyed over her. It's not going to change anything.

"Ready, Ryle?"

I look back at her to see her drop her hand on Ryle's head. He nods, but he climbs up the bleachers to hug me.

"Bye, Dad."

I watch them walk away, wondering when he stopped calling me *Daddy*. The saddest thing about that is I've been gone so much in his childhood, I didn't hear *daddy* nearly enough.

CHAPTER TEN

TRUMAN

Ethan chatters nonstop on the drive home. First, he's all caught up in the excitement of the ball game. He does almost a play-by-play commentary for a few minutes. I'm impressed that he paid that much attention to the game, and I wonder what, if anything, Ryle is saying to Julie. Ethan switches topics so smoothly, I almost don't even realize it when he starts talking about Harper and Keith. Apparently, my sister is not being a good patient, and her husband is not happy with her.

Again, I think about Ryle and wonder about the things he says when he's with my parents or Julie's parents. What things he might have said to his teacher. Then again, Julie's his custodial parent, and I'm not sure I've ever done anything crazy for him to share at school.

I walk Ethan inside when we get to Harper's house. He's still talking, but he's totally lost me now. I'm nodding along with him like I'm following what he's saying, but he's talking about *Minecraft* in one breath and *Mario* in the next, and I'm pretty sure he mixed in something about *The Lego Movie*. I'm not sure Ryle has ever said this many words in his life.

He's still talking when he pushes the front door open and bounds inside. I close the door behind me and holler at Ethan when he skips right by the living room where Harper is spending her time these days. Ethan skids to a stop in the hall and looks back at me curiously.

"Aren't you going to say hi to your mom?" I nod my head toward the living room. "Tell her about your game?"

"Oh." He looks pained to have to slow down and talk to her, but by the time he's in the living room with her, he's taken a breath and started yakking all over again. Harper looks from Ethan, perched on the edge of the couch by her feet, to me when I drop quietly into the chair just inside the doorway.

I offer her a silent smile and watch her turn her attention back to Ethan. He rattles on for another five minutes, and then he stops and turns sideways to study her toes peeking out from her cast.

"Can I watch TV?" he asks her, his eyes still on her toes.

"For a half hour," she answers. "I'll have Hattie come and get you. You need a bath."

"Why?"

I snort at his whine but school my features into a blank mask when he glances at me.

"Maybe because it looks like you brought half the dirt on

the field home with you?" Harper shrugs. "Actually, you should take a bath now and then watch TV for a little bit."

"Mo-om." Ethan rolls his eyes.

"Want me to help him?" I ask her. My mind wants to drag me down memory lane, when I helped my son get ready for bed just a few nights ago.

"No, thanks," Harper says with a small smile. "Craig'll help."

I wonder if that's wise. Craig would probably be more likely to try and drown his little brother in the shower than help him with something. But Ethan climbs to his feet, bumping Harper's cast as he does. She grits her teeth but turns the grimace into a smile when Ethan flashes her a guilty look.

"I'm sorry."

"It's okay." She holds her fist out for a knuckle bump, which my nephew gives her with a big grin. He turns to me as he walks out of the room and thanks me for the ride home.

"You okay?" I ask the second we're alone. "Did that hurt?"

"I'll live." She rests her head on the pillow propped behind her back and closes her eyes. "This is making me nuts, Truman."

"I know." I do know. Harper is one of those people who is always on the move. Sitting still like this has to be hard on her. "At least you can work from home."

"True." She slits her eyes open and stares at me. My sister looks tired. It's not a look I've seen on her too often, and less so since she got out of college and joined Mom and Dad in the business. "How was the game?"

"Fun." I shrug. "The coach had Ethan on first for a bit."

"Julie sent me a few pictures."

"Yeah, I saw that."

"How come you brought Ethan home?"

Not sure why it matters, I narrow my eyes at Harper and shrug. "I offered."

"Was Julie put out that I asked her to drive Ethan?"

"Not at all." I shake my head.

"Okay." Harper nods. But from the way she's looking at me, I can tell she has more on her mind. More about me and Julie.

"What?"

"It's just too bad you and Julie don't do these things together."

"We sat together at the game, Harp." I hope I sound casual, because I feel anything but, and I don't want to have this conversation with anyone, least of all Harper.

"But you should have driven to the game together. You should be there with her and Ryle now. At home."

I should be. If I hadn't been so selfish when she told me she was pregnant, things might be different.

"I was supposed to be in Miami this week."

"Oh, I know." The sharp edge in her tone makes me sit up straighter. Is she mad at me for skipping out on the travel?

"I didn't want to miss his first game," I confess.

"Good."

"It's a lot."

"Being a dad?"

"Being on the road all the time."

"Truman, you don't have to be gone all the time. That's why we have employees. And Zoom meetings."

I know that. But part of me worries that Julie won't be happy with me if I end up around here more often. Sure, she'll let me see Ryle, but what happens if I cut my travel way back and want to spend more time with him through the week? That'll cut into her time with him.

I clear my throat and nod. "I know."

"Do you still love her?"

Harper and I have always been close without being close enough that we talk about feelings like this. Uncomfortable with the thought of anyone prying into my business, it's hard to look my sister in the eye right now.

"Truman?"

"Yeah, Harper, I still love her," I say as I jump out of the chair like someone lit a fire under my butt. "Do you need anything? Pain pill?"

"Does she know?" Harper totally ignores my attempt to change the subject.

"No." I shrug, drag my eyes around the room, and eventually meet her gaze. "Doesn't matter."

"Of course it matters, Truman!" She plants her hands down on the cushions and uses them to push herself up to sit straighter. "You have a child with her. If you love her, you need to tell her. Neither of you are getting any younger, and neither of you has settled down with anyone else—"

"I'm not even thirty," I remind her.

"But you're not happy with what you're doing," she argues. "I dunno. Maybe at first, living big and crazy and all the travel and women were your thing."

"Harper," I grind her name out through clenched teeth.

"But even if that was the case—"

"It's not the case," I snap. "It's never been the case. I've always been in love with Julie, and no matter how I've tried to get over her, I can't."

"Then tell her." She shrugs.

I stare at my sister for a moment and finally shake my head. "I'll be gone for a few—"

"Did you cheat?"

Her soft-spoken question stops me at the doorway. I'm sure it's what everyone thinks—Truman cheated on Julie, and she broke things off. Still, hearing someone ask, hearing someone who's supposed to be on my side say those words, cuts through me like a dull blade.

"No." With my back to her, I huff out a long, tired sigh. "I didn't, Harp. See ya in a few days."

CHAPTER ELEVEN

Julie

"That's adorable." Dani clutches my phone in her hand and scrolls through the pictures I took at Ryle's first ball game. "I hate that I had to miss it."

"Morning sickness can do that to you."

"At six in the evening."

I take my phone back and smile in commiseration. "Everyone's pregnancy is different, Dani. Don't beat yourself up over it."

"When's his next game?"

"Tomorrow night."

"Great. I'll be there." Dani nods. "I'm glad you talked to Truman about getting Ryle signed up."

I freeze at the mention of Truman's name. Eyes locked with Dani's, I can't play it off and pretend like it had no effect on me.

"What?" she asks. Her smile fades a bit.

"What?" I take a sip of my tea and shrug nonchalantly, but that only makes her more suspicious.

"What's going on with you and Truman?"

"Nothing," I answer truthfully. "He's out of town."

"Breaking news." She rolls her eyes. "But seriously. You had this look on your face."

I can fight this for an hour or two or give in and tell her about Truman being around the other night. She always liked him, but she's always supported me since we broke up.

In the beginning, I thought I would never forgive him. Sometimes now, I think I have, but that doesn't mean being around him, parenting Ryle with him, and not being *with* him doesn't hurt.

"That day I took Ryle to see Harper?"

Dani nods, eyes narrowed at me now like she's expecting me to share some deep, dark secret.

"Truman brought Ryle home that night. He stayed for dinner."

"And?" She leans over the table and stares at me. The look is so dangerous, I sit back and look around the café. We're on our lunch breaks—Dani needs to get back to her job at City Hall, and I need to get back to the bank. Talking to my best friend is usually much more fun than crunching numbers, but today, I think I'm ready to jump from my chair and run back to work.

"And nothing." I shrug. "Ryle wanted him to stay. So he did. He and Ryle played games while I got things cleaned up. And then he helped Ryle get ready for bed."

Dani winces. "Oh no. Ryle's got his hopes up now? He thinks Truman's going to be around like that more often?" She nods in understanding, but she stops suddenly and tips her head at me when she realizes I'm not nodding along. "Julie?"

"Ryle actually did really well with it," I tell her. "I worried he might get upset after the game. He came home with me, but he gave Truman a hug goodbye. Truman took Ethan home."

Dani bites her lip and lowers her gaze to the table between us.

"Are you sure about this, Jules?" she whispers. "After everything?"

"No," I admit quickly, "I'm not. I'm just...He's been around more lately. And he's so good with Ryle."

Dani sighs and looks up at me. "What can I do?"

"I don't know. I guess this baseball thing wasn't such a good idea for me. We both want to be out there watching Ryle, but I don't think I can see him a few times a week. It's too much."

"You guys could trade games?"

I shake my head and start stacking my dishes and trash. "Not fair to Ryle."

"You could wear a suit of armor."

"He didn't ravish me, Dani." I roll my eyes. "We talked."

"About?"

"Nothing important."

Dani groans softly. "That's dangerous."

"Getting along with him?"

"Mmm." She nods. "I'll be at the game tomorrow night. I'll run interference."

I laugh as we stand and collect our things. "I'm not even sure he'll be there tomorrow."

"Well, I'll be ready if he is. I can play defense." She pats her still flat belly. "Give me a bit and I'll be big like a linebacker."

"You'll never be that big, and that's football."

She giggles and throws her arm around my shoulders as we walk outside together.

"Hey." She squeezes me before she lets go. "Eric offered to send us to Florida for a beach getaway before the baby's here, and my life's upside down. What do you think?"

"A girls' getaway to the beach?" I smile and nod. "I think that sounds perfect!"

My worries over Ryle and his getting too attached to Truman don't pan out for a number of reasons. As the weeks go by, Truman is around sometimes, but not always. He's at some games, but not all of them. Ryle spends more and more time at Harper's house, and now that Twain is seeing Mabry, Ryle spends some time with them and Mabry's nephew.

And Truman seems to be avoiding me. He's back to walking Ryle to the door on the rare occasions when he brings him home. He's polite to me, and he always seems genuinely happy to be with Ryle, but something's changed between us yet again. Ryle never mentions the dinner thing. He doesn't talk about that night, and he doesn't ask if Truman can come again.

Which tells me anything I might have been thinking about me and Truman was all in my head. He's probably got women at his beck and call in every state, and the last thing he would want is to settle down with someone like me.

I mean, he said as much when I was pregnant. I'm the one who had stars in her eyes this time around and read too much into my ex being nice.

"Hey!" The excitement is real when I see Harper at my door. She's on crutches, but she's got a new cast. This one is smaller and maybe a bit more manageable.

"Hi." She offers me a weak grin.

"How's it feeling?"

She stares at me for a moment, thinking it over. Usually put together like a million bucks, her hair is disheveled, and she's wearing a simple t-shirt with sporty shorts. She looks harried and pale, still.

"Little better," she decides. "But it's exhausting."

Behind me, I hear Ryle and Ethan playing down the hall. Ethan spent the night; the boys and I had a little pizza party last night, and we watched *Cars*. I had them in bed with lights out by nine, but I heard a lot of giggling coming from Ryle's room even after that.

"Did you drive here?" I lean way out the door to look around, but I don't see any cars.

"No." She laughs. "I wish. Keith dropped me off. He's getting the oil changed in his car. Then he'll be back for us."

"Oh." I nod and step out of the way to give her room to come inside.

"Do you mind if I hang out with you for a while?"

"Of course not."

I don't mind, though I'm a little flustered. I don't spend that much time with anyone in Truman's family. I've probably been around Twain more than any of them, just because Ryle likes to go to the skating rink and drive the go-karts at Wolverine Park.

"Thanks."

Harper moves with grace into the kitchen, but I've done crutches and casts, and I know it's work. I'm sure her foot still hurts, and I know the crutches make her armpits sore.

"Want something to drink?"

She lifts her chin and stares at me like I've offered her a trip to Disneyland. "Please tell me you have wine."

I do, but I wonder if she should be drinking.

"Should you be drinking, Harper?"

"You sound like my brothers." She groans. "I'm not on pain meds. I took Tylenol about six hours ago."

"If they find out I gave you wine, I'll be in trouble with the whole family."

"Except me. And I'm the boss," she reminds me.

That does it. We share a laugh as I grab two wine glasses from the cabinet and take a bottle of Sauvignon Blanc from the refrigerator.

"Do you want to sit in here? Will you be comfortable?"

"Yeah, it's fine."

"The boys ate lunch a while ago," I announce as I pour the wine. I turn as she's lowering herself to a chair. Once she's sitting, I pull another chair up for her to prop her leg on. She mumbles her thanks and takes the wine I offer. I watch her lift the glass and drink deeply.

"Rough times." I snag my own glass from the counter and sit down across from her.

She snorts and pinches the bridge of her nose. "I hate not being in the office. I don't know how Twain can stand it."

Twain is a bit of a mystery. Super sweet guy, same good looks as Harper and Truman, but the killer business gene apparently skipped over Twain and went right from Harper to Truman. The Woolff amusement park is all his, and that's all he wants to deal with. He's laid back and happy as a lamb to be outdoors. I've heard he's more like some lost uncle than his own parents.

"I think I could use a break from the office," I admit as I

sweep my hand over the table toward her cast. "But maybe not like that."

"It's not that bad," she mumbles. "It doesn't throb like it did at first."

"That's good."

"Ethan wanted to decorate it for me."

Of course Ethan would want to decorate her cast. And of course Harper would never allow it.

"It would be one of a kind."

She laughs softly. "True." She sips her wine again, and I'm relieved this drink is much smaller than the first one.

"Have you seen Truman?" she asks casually. I'm a bit suspicious of why she's asking, because I haven't seen him to talk to him other than saying hi at the games.

"Not for several days. I assumed he was out of town."

Harper tips her head and frowns. "I don't think so."

At a loss for something to say, I take a drink.

"It's weird," I tell her and then wish immediately that I would have kept my mouth shut.

"What's weird?"

I nibble on my lip, considering how to answer her. "He said he wanted to be around more, and he was for a while."

"And now he's not?"

He is, though. My face floods with heat when I realize he's been around for Ryle. They've spent a lot of time together this summer. Truman just hasn't been around as much to talk to me lately. Which is totally okay since we're just two polite adults raising our son together.

Before I can figure out what to say to Harper, Ethan and Ryle explode into the kitchen, giggling and yelling about a game. Relieved at the interruption, I jump up to get them a snack, but I feel Harper's eyes on me the whole time.

CHAPTER TWELVE

Truman

Apparently, Harper invited Jules to my mom's birthday dinner. I can't argue about it; after all, Harper always does the dinner at her house. Even this year, when she's still hobbling around in the kitchen and should probably be resting, she's hosting Mom's birthday dinner. She has plenty of help—even Mabry keeps insisting that she wants to do something for Harper.

Mom seems happy to see Jules when she and Ryle appear on Harper's deck, so that makes me happy, too. But it feels like Harper has an agenda, and when she starts sneaking peeks at me as soon as Julie shows up, it doesn't even feel like a hidden agenda.

It's weird now to be around Julie, too. I've been in love with her for years, but I've never admitted it to anyone. Now that I've said it out loud to Harper, now that my sister's asked me if I cheated on Jules and drove her away, all the things between Julie and me are back again—the good and the bad.

All the fun times, but all the arguments, too. Including the big one that blew us apart. Ryle sees me sitting at the patio table and comes over to climb into my lap.

"Dad!" He twists around to look me in the eyes. "Mom took me to the batting cage!"

The batting cage? The only batting cage I know about has three pitching machines: slow pitch, fast ball, and really fast ball. Surely, Julie wouldn't put him in that fast ball cage? He's only six.

"Ryle!"

Ethan and Mabry's nephew Bryson thump up the deck steps and make a beeline for my lap. Both of them join Ryle there, and the three of them put their heads together to conspire. I feel someone watching me, and I assume it's Harper. But when the boys jump from my lap and scramble back across the deck to the steps, I realize it's Julie.

She's got a drink in her hand. I would've gotten her something, but I was talking to our son. I wish he hadn't run off so soon. I know it's better for him to be down and playing with the other boys, but I would have liked more details on his trip to the batting cages.

We make eye contact, but before either of us can even smile at each other—though I'm not sure I could find a smile for her after that—my mom sweeps in and throws her arms around her. Something so simple. Mom's a hugger; she's always been that way. She'd hug the bank teller if she could get behind the counter.

I haven't had my arms around Julie since that night we broke up. I wasn't there when Ryle was born; after everything was said and done, she didn't want me there. It's my biggest regret as far as my son is concerned. My regrets with Julie could fill a book.

I turn away and reach for my longneck only to find it empty. I stand as I snag the bottle to go find another.

"Beer me, too," Twain tells me as I pass by the grill where he, Dad, and Keith are parked, discussing the new John Deere tractor he bought for his land by the park. I snatch his empty bottle with a growl and go inside to find Harper in the kitchen.

"What're you doing?"

Caught in the act, she shoots me a sheepish grin. At the counter, she's reaching for something in a cabinet over her head. One crutch is propped against the counter. The other, thankfully, is tucked precariously under her arm.

"I need that serving platter."

Frustrated with her both because she's going to hurt herself and because she's sticking her nose in where it doesn't belong with Jules and me, I frown at her and toss the empty bottles in the recycle can before going to help her.

"What would you have done if your crutch had fallen?" I turn to her when I put the platter on the counter for her.

"I guess I'd have waited in here for you to come and save me."

"And what if I don't feel like saving you?"

"You just did," she said with a smile. "Don't be silly."

Afraid she's going to either fall or drop the serving platter, I snatch it when she tries to pick it up.

"What do you need done with this?"

"Why are you so grouchy?"

Both crutches under her arms again, she moves over to the fridge and opens it.

"I have cheese to put out."

"Move." I shoo her away from the refrigerator, find the cheese, and carry it back to the platter. She stands at my side as I arrange the cheeses on the platter.

"Nope." She shakes her head and tugs the platter closer so she can correct the cheese layout. When I catch her peeking at me, I roll my eyes. "Like this."

"It's cheese, Harper," I tell her. "No one cares."

I'm being mean. While I'm irritated that Harper has suddenly decided to make me a project, I am glad Julie's here. I think. On the other hand, it's hard to talk to her around all the bad vibes in my head, and it's hard to avoid her when she's here with my family for my mom.

The thing is, Harper and Keith throw a nice party. Keith is a true grill master. Harper's fancy—the table is decked out with bouquets of flowers and a fancy cake. Harper's got a cute stack of fancy paper plates and matching napkins. Small dishes of candies. She's always over the top, and although no one expects her to do so much, we all enjoy it and appreciate it.

"I get it," she says quietly, eyes back on the cheese. "You're mad at me."

"Me and Julie aren't your business."

I don't know why I expect her to back off. She takes a deep breath, finishes arranging the cheese slices, and then hobbles back to the fridge.

"What now?"

"Grapes."

I lean into the fridge and find a bowl of grapes. She watches me put it on the counter.

"You're my little brother."

I nod. "And if you and Keith were having problems, would you be okay with me nosing around?"

"I'm not nosing around."

"You're spending more time with Julie than I do. What's that about? Why is she here today?"

Harper has the grace to look chagrined when I call her out on how much time she's been spending with my ex. I know they're hanging out at the ball games. That's not such a big deal. But Ryle mentioned something one day about Harper being at the house all the time. I have no doubt he's exaggerating, but there has to be something to base that on.

"Did you know Dani's pregnant?"

Dani is Julie's best friend. I used to know her and Eric, her husband, well. I haven't talked to either of them in years.

"No."

Harper nods as she pops a grape into her mouth.

"Did you know Eric's cousin is moving to Bassett?"

"What?"

Did Julie tell me that? She said Dani wanted to set them up that weekend a while back, when we first got Ryle signed up for tee-ball. But I'm pretty sure she didn't mention anything about Jerad moving to Bassett.

"And since Dani and Eric are now going to be out of the social network for a while, they're all going to Florida together."

"All—what—?"

Harper meets my eyes and shrugs. "She asked me if Ryle could stay here."

"What did you tell her?"

"What else would I tell her, but yes, Truman? After all, if you're not gonna fight for her by now, you're not gonna fight for her. What's a trip to Florida with some other guy mean to you?"

CHAPTER THIRTEEN

JULIE

Truman disappears into the house while I'm talking to his mom. Normally, I would be okay with that, but today is different. We haven't talked much lately, he didn't look thrilled to see me when I walked out here with Ryle, and he's been in the house for a long time. Maybe he has a girlfriend here. In fact, maybe he went inside to catch her before she came outside. But he knows I won't care. Well, I mean, we're over and have been for years, so it's not like he has to hide his dates from me.

"Hey!" Twain's girlfriend, Mabry, gives me a one-armed hug. She's holding a tray of crackers and olives in her free hand. "How's it going, Julie?"

"Great, thanks." I nod and reach across her to grab a cracker. Interesting. This is the first time in a very long time I've been invited to anything involving Truman's family. It's obvious he's not happy I'm here; apparently, that's why I don't get many invites.

Mabry's a perfect fit for Truman's older brother, Twain. She's about as laid back and fun as Twain is. If she and I could spend more time together, I'm pretty sure we'd be the kind of friends who share margaritas, laughter, and secrets.

"Do you—"

"Jules."

Truman's harsh tone booms over Mabry. I glance to my left when I feel his fingers dig into my upper arm. What the heck did I do to make him angry with me? Once we had it out and broke up, we promised not to fight, not to take potshots at each other. For Ryle's sake. That promise has worked for six years. Why is he suddenly snipping at me?

"I'll talk to you later, Julie." Mabry offers me a smile, narrows her eyes at Truman in a sneer that makes me laugh, and slips away from us.

"What's up?" I turn my full attention to Truman, but I'm still laughing at Mabry. That only makes Truman look grouchier.

"Can we talk for a second?"

"Sure." I shrug and follow him when he leads the way back into the house. We don't stop in the kitchen, as I expected. He doesn't even stop in the living room. In fact, he marches me right out to the front porch. He pulls the door closed behind us and then stares at me with a severe frown. "If you don't want me here, I can go."

He draws back like I slapped him, but he still doesn't say anything.

"Harper invited me, Truman."

He twists and paces over the porch and then stands with his back to me.

"Truman?"

"Did you take Ryle to the batting cages?"

His question throws me off. Yes, I took Ryle to the batting cages. I have no idea why that's a problem for Truman.

I nod when he glances at me and wait for him to say more.

"Seriously?" He spins around and throws his hands up. "Do you know how hard—"

"Wait." I shake my head and put my hand up to stop him. When he stays where he is, I cross the porch to stand closer to him. "Really? You're judging my parenting?"

"Jules, that's hardcore—"

"He didn't bat, Truman!" I snap, indignant with anger. How dare he question anything I do with my son? Truman might be his father, but he didn't want him in the early days, and I am Ryle's custodial parent.

"What?"

"Do you really think I would put him in a cage with a fastball coming at him at ninety miles per hour?" I tip my head and study his face. "Did Ryle tell you I let him get in a cage?"

Truman's hesitation only makes me madder. "No."

"So, you just assumed I would do that? Because what? I'm too dumb to know how hard the machines throw? Or I'm neglectful and don't care?"

"Whoa, whoa, Jules." Truman shakes his head and steps back. "It's not—"

"It is like that. You just came at me, guns blazing, for something you assumed."

He's frustrated—with me, yes, but now, more with himself.

"How dare you judge my parenting."

"Julie—"

I'm spoiling for a fight. The realization almost knocks the wind out of me. It's been years since I've been on the receiving end of Truman Woolff's passion, and even if it's anger now rather than love, I like it. I've missed the way he's looking at me right now.

"If it were up to you—"

He cuts me off with a growl. "Yeah, yeah, I know. If it were up to me, Ryle wouldn't be here. Will you ever let that go?"

"Let it go?" I step closer to him, and even I hear my voice jump an octave and a decibel or two. "Let it go? When have I ever brought that up—"

"You ended everything we had because of that!" Truman yells loudly enough that I wonder if anyone in the back can hear him. He doesn't look angry, though. Not anymore. His face is a mask of pain. I recognize it, because it's a look I see in the mirror now and then.

"I did," I agree quietly. "But I've never brought it up again."

Truman takes a deep breath, and all the fight goes out of him. His shoulders slump, and he ducks his head.

"You're going to Florida?"

"What?" Confused when he changes the subject, I can only stare at him and try to catch up.

"With Dani and Eric?"

How does he know that? I know for a fact Dani didn't tell him. Dani wouldn't blow him off if she saw him, but she certainly wouldn't share the fact that we're going to Florida, either.

"Yeah."

"And Eric's cousin?"

Truman's voice breaks the slightest bit, and it hits me that Harper has been at the house a few times recently. It's usually under the guise of getting the boys together, but I wonder now if there's more to it. I mentioned to her once or twice about going to the beach now since Dani won't be free to do that for a while once the baby comes. I don't remember saying anything about Jerad going, but I suppose I might have referenced him at some point.

"What? Why does it matter?"

"Is he going?"

"No."

"Dani's trying to set you up with him."

"What difference does that make to you?" I ask him rather than assuring him it won't happen.

"Jules." Truman sighs as he steps closer to me. We're standing much too close together now. If any of his family saw us like this, we would have some explaining to do. Not sure what to think of this, of Truman's sudden objection to my seeing anyone else, I step backwards and toss out something to drive him away.

"We took Ryle to the batting cages."

"We? You? You and Jerad?"

Interesting that he remembers Jerad's name.

"The four of us," I correct him. I might be trying to push him away, but I don't want to hurt him. I don't want Truman to worry that there's a special guy in my life who might be a threat to his relationship with Ryle.

"The four of you."

I nod. "Eric and Jerad were in the cages. Ryle just watched."

"Nice." Truman tucks his hands in his pockets. A little sliver of regret needles me when I see the flash of hurt on his face. Now we stand together on the porch with six years of buried hard feelings between us.

"I was going to kiss you just now." He meets my eyes, and that little sliver of regret is a knife in my throat.

If he had kissed me, I would have kissed him back. As much as it hurts, it's better that I broke the moment.

"I know."

CHAPTER FOURTEEN

Truman

She doesn't make a scene. She doesn't storm out of here without saying goodbye to anyone. My ex has too much class for that. Instead, she stares at me a moment longer and then turns and goes back into Harper's house.

Feeling like an idiot for how I handled that—it's becoming a theme for me and how I communicate with Julie—I linger on the front porch a bit. I don't even know what I'm so angry about. Yes, I would have been outraged if Julie had let Ryle get in a batting cage. But, did I really believe that she would do that?

No.

Was that anger, that sudden need to confront her more about me just needing to get close enough to her to argue with her?

Harper's well-timed jab about Julie going to Florida with her friends did exactly what it was supposed to do, whether that's see red, see green, or ride a wave of regret and despair I'll never get off. No matter what—if I don't tell Jules how I feel about her now, she'll end up in love with someone else.

And what kind of man would I be to waltz in and take that away from her?

I'm in love with her, yes. But she's cool as a cucumber—unless I'm slinging baseless accusations at her—and she makes me feel like a bumbling idiot. I know I could and should have handled that discussion better. I'm a businessman, a professional, and yet, I let my crush rattle me all the time.

She's not just a crush, though. The stakes are so much higher than that, including my son's happiness. I hear the front door open and look over my shoulder when Twain sticks his head out.

"You okay?"

I figure Harper sent him out here to check on me. Not because she's afraid to confront me again. But because he's much more mobile at the moment. I answer him with a curt nod. I have no desire to talk to anyone right now about anything, most especially either of my siblings about my ex-girlfriend.

Twain studies me for a second. To make sure he gets the message that I don't want to talk, I look back at the front yard. Harper's lawn is immaculate. Just like the rest of her life—usually. Just like Twain and Mabry's life together now.

I wonder if I'll be the only Woolff to have a messy, less than perfect life.

Twain takes the hint and leaves me alone. But I know if I don't show my face on the deck again, Harper will crutch her way out to the porch, and *she* won't take a hint and leave me alone.

When I go back to the deck, everything's as it should be. Keith is still manning the grill—currently, Ethan is helping him. Twain and Dad are out in the yard with Ryle and Bryson. I watch Twain lob a whiffle ball at Ryle. A little thrill of pride tingles in me when Ryle whops it back at him.

Harper is finally sitting down, but she's at the table with Mabry, Mom, and Jules. Julie's hand is wrapped around a longneck, and she wears a sweet smile. She's looking Mom's way, but the second she turns her head and meets my eyes, the smile freezes. As much as I want to go to her and talk, I know better. I'd only say something else stupid. And as much as it hurts to see her hanging out with my family when she and I can't get it right, I don't want to chase her away.

Instead of joining them, I head out to the yard to play ball with the boys. Twain gives me a look, but he keeps his mouth shut. Ryle high fives me, and then Bryson's up to bat. Ethan runs out to join us, and then Craig and Hattie appear out of nowhere, and we have a ball game.

The carefree play with the kids is what I needed. I forget that Jules is here, and that I once told her I didn't want to have children this young. I forget that she cut me off and that I still love her, and I have fun with my family. The game gets hardcore, so by the time Keith announces that the burgers are done, I'm glad for the break. I linger at the base of the deck while the ladies and then the kids fix their plates, and then finally, I grab a burger and some sides. I'm not hungry, but I know Harper's watching my every move right now, and she's cataloging everything to grill me on later.

Julie sits at the patio table again with Mom, Mabry, and Harper. So I hang out on the opposite end of the deck with Twain, Keith, and Dad. I don't know if anyone else feels it, but I can hardly breathe, the tension between me and Jules is so thick.

She stays long enough to have cake, and she gives Mom a present. It's a pale yellow scarf, and I hear her say Ryle picked it out. Mom raves over it, but she's sincere, and I know she likes the scarf, and she loves that Ryle chose it for her. The second the gifts are all open, Julie says her goodbyes and stands to leave.

I don't want her to leave yet, but considering the fact that we've avoided each other most of the evening, it would be weird to protest her leaving now. Instead, I cut her off at the deck steps, assuming she's going to collect Ryle and go home.

"Don't." I keep plenty of space between us. Not because my family might be watching now, but because I don't trust myself. I still want to kiss her. Maybe even more so after the little squabble on the porch—the first we've had since we broke up. Since watching her interact with my family. Hearing her laughter from across the deck.

"Don't what?" she asks quietly.

"Let him stay. I'll bring him home later."

She stares at me long enough that I think she might argue.
The part of me that wants her to argue is disappointed
when she finally nods and takes a step back from me. If she
argued, we could stand here toe-to-toe longer—so close I
smell her soft, sweet scent. Same thing she's always worn. I
have to shove down the memories of curling up with her on
the sofa to watch movies, burying my face in her hair.

"Just gonna tell him goodbye," she mumbles as she walks
away from me.

I watch from where I'm standing as Julie lifts her fist to Ryle
for a knuckle tap. My son's giggle carries over the yard. I
wonder what he thinks of Eric's cousin hanging around
them all of the sudden. He's young, but he's a smart kid, and
he notices things. Not to mention, kids in general aren't left
to be kids for long these days.

What do I know? Maybe he likes Jerad.

"Why did you ask Harper to watch him?" I fall into step
beside Julie when she approaches me. We walk around the
side of the house rather than up to the deck and through the
house.

Julie shoots me a look as we round the house, and I stay with
her as she walks to her car.

"I don't want to do this with you, Truman." She folds her
arms over her chest when we stand at her car. "Not here."

"I'm just saying I'm right here. And I'm his dad."

"And sometimes you travel," she reminds me.

"Not as much lately."

She nods. "I know. But still." She shrugs. "Besides, Harper offered. We thought the boys would have fun together."

Of course the boys will have fun together. But that's not the point. She could have asked me to keep our son while she's gone.

"When are you going?"

"It's not even set in stone, Truman," she says quietly. "We're talking about it. Looking at dates."

"I thought you weren't into Jerad." I'm pressing my luck jumping subjects. I have the right to ask her about Ryle, to ask her why she didn't ask me if he could stay with me when she's gone. I don't have the right to ask her about Jerad or anyone else she might date.

She stares at me silently and finally shakes her head.

"I'll see you later." She glances at me as she pulls her car door open. Once again, I'm left standing and watching her drive away.

I take my time going back inside. The one nice thing about traveling so much is that I don't have time to think about Julie. And it's not just because I meet and date other women. The meetings, the walk-throughs on the potential purchases, the discussions about remodels—everything I do keeps my mind busy and focused.

But being too busy to think about Julie means I'm too busy to be with Ryle.

And I want to be around more to spend as much time as I can with Ryle.

Which means I'm around Julie more, which means she's on my mind more.

Harper's in the kitchen when I go back inside. Standing at the counter with her crutches, she looks like she's been waiting there to confront me. I bite back a sigh when Twain slips in the back door, too.

"What happened?" Harper demands.

"I told her I'd bring Ryle—"

"What happened that split you up?" She lifts her chin and stares at me defiantly. There's the woman I know from the boardroom, not from the house where we grew up together. "What is going on with you two, Truman?"

I glance from her to Twain, who's now leaning over the end of the counter, watching me with the same fierce look.

"You said you didn't cheat—"

"I did not cheat!" I snap and yell as the back door opens again. Mom steps inside with Ethan. She looks at each of us, all frozen in mid-conversation, and then drops her hand on Ethan's shoulder to spin him around and march him back outside.

"But, Grandma!" Ethan argues. "You said we could—"

Mom pulls the door closed, leaving me with my siblings. And the thought that whenever this inquisition is over, Mom's going to demand to know what's going on.

"Then what?" Harper fires away.

"I think what Harper means is that it's obvious to anyone who watches you that you're in love with Julie."

"And she's in love with you," Harper says softly. "And you're wasting time, and you're depriving your son of a central family unit—"

She stops talking when I pinch the bridge of my nose and shake my head.

"You guys know Julie's family." I put it out there as a reminder, not a question. Julie has two brothers. They're the golden sons. One of them actually served time for drunk driving, but the minute he got out of prison, Julie's dad handed him the keys to a new house and a job at the family law firm. The other brother is the principal of some swanky academy for rich kids.

Julie's dad had no use for a girl. She's never been close to him, though she grew up under the same roof where he and her brothers lived. She's usually on speaking terms with her mother, but now and then, things go sideways between them, too, as her mom caters to her dad and her brothers.

"You broke up with her because of her family?" Twain asks with a frown.

"She has two brothers." Harper's eyes search my face for more clues, but she comes up empty and simply shrugs.

"She's not close to her dad."

"Okay?" Harper arches her eyebrows, obviously still not following me.

"Like, her dad didn't want a daughter. Has no use for her."

"Well, he's a jerk," Harper says and shrugs, as if it's obvious. "But that shouldn't have any bearing on the two of you."

I glance at Twain. This part is harder. This part is all about me being a selfish jerk. Too immature to step up and be responsible.

"When Jules told me she was pregnant," I mumble and turn away from my siblings. I feel the weight of their stares on my back as I pace through the room. "I didn't want a baby. Wasn't ready to be a dad."

"So..." Twain clears his throat. "You just left her high and dry to deal with the pregnancy on her own?"

"What made you change your mind about Ryle?"

"I didn't just leave her." Ignoring Harper's question, I swallow hard, a knot of emotion in my throat. Turning back to them, I slide onto a stool at the bar and scrub my hands over my head. "I didn't want to lose her. I just didn't want a baby."

"Oh, Truman." Harper winces.

"I suggested she have an abortion. That we stay together. And maybe we could have kids later."

"Oh boy." Twain groans.

"Doesn't work that way," Harper whispers. "Julie had a *baby* growing inside her. A baby she *wanted*. Because she loves you."

"I know."

"I mean, if *she* hadn't been ready...that's one thing. But asking her to abort your baby so you could play a little longer?"

I jerk my gaze up from the granite counter to meet my sister's eyes. "Yeah, I know."

"Put you right in the same category her dad and brothers are in."

I nod.

"So." I cough a little to hack that emotion out of my throat and then take a deep breath. "Now you know why she'll never forgive me. And why we'll never be together."

CHAPTER FIFTEEN

JULIE

Ryle looks like a bedraggled puppy when Truman brings him home. He steps inside and leans into me with a yawn.

"Are you tired?" I smooth my hand over his hair and note the milk mustache on his face when he tips his head up to look at me. When he nods, I look back at Truman, who honestly looks even worse than Ryle. It's late enough that I send Ryle straight to the shower. Once Ryle's in the bathroom, I turn back to Truman.

"Thanks for letting him stay for a while," he says quietly. His hands are in his pockets, his shoulders slouched. "Goodnight—"

"Truman." I reach for him but catch myself before I actually touch him. "Look. I think we need to clear the air."

He quirks his eyebrows at me and clears his throat.

"I'm sorry. I've been a jerk lately. Just..." He shrugs. "I have some stuff on my mind—"

"Will you come in? Please?"

He ducks his chin and steps inside.

"Let me just check on Ryle. I'll be right back."

With a silent nod, he leans on the counter by the stove, and I move quickly down the hall to check on Ryle. I find him in the bathroom, already in his pjs, brushing his teeth.

"I don't want to shower," he tells me as he leans over the sink to spit. "Can I just do it in the morning?"

"Sure." I brush his hair back again, a little bit sad when he ducks away from me. "What'd you do at Aunt Harper's?"

"Played whiffle ball," he answers.

"Again? Who won?"

"Grandma, Mabry, Craig, and Bryson."

"You and Dad lost, huh?"

"Dad didn't play." Ryle shakes his head as he puts his toothbrush back in the holder and wipes his mouth off with the hand towel. "He was grouchy."

Ryle doesn't say things like that often. Knowing that whatever is going on between me and Truman right now is affecting the way Truman treats Ryle makes me feel guilty.

"Maybe he's just tired," I suggest. Truman did say he has a lot on his mind right now. Maybe his moody behavior has nothing to do with me.

"Goodnight, Mom."

I follow Ryle into his room and wait while he gets comfortable in his bed before I pull his sheet and quilt up over him. At least he still lets me kiss him goodnight. I know a day will come when he won't want me to do that anymore.

Truman's standing right where I left him when I go back in the kitchen.

"No shower?" He moves only to fold his arms over his chest.

"Said he's too tired."

"He did play hard." Truman nods.

"He also said you were grouchy."

I'm teasing him, but the look on his face suggests he takes me seriously.

"Like I said," he shrugs, "lot on my mind."

"Truman, I was teasing."

We lock gazes, and seconds tick away as we stare at each other.

"Look." I lick my lips and pull out a chair to sit down. Rather than look at Truman, I fold my hands on the table and stare at my short, bare nails. "I don't know how to say this, so I'm just going to do it fast and get it over with."

"Say what?"

"I feel like something's changed between us this summer. And the only thing that's really different is that you've been around more."

"So, you want me to go back to traveling more?"

"I didn't say that." I shake my head at him. "You're good at that, ya know?"

"Good at what?" He moves away from the counter and sits at the table across from me.

"Reading into everything I say to you."

"I want to spend more time with Ryle."

"Okay."

"But I worry that'll be a problem for you."

"When have I ever said I didn't want you around him?"

"You haven't, but I still only see him on the weekends. Or weeknights at his games."

"All you have to do is tell me, Truman."

"Okay."

"There's something else."

He looks surprised again.

"I feel like part of this is my fault."

"Part of what?"

"The tension between us."

"Look, if you're into Jerad, it's not my business. You deserve to be happy, Jules."

"There it is again." I tilt my head and study his face. I used to be able to read him so easily. Now when I look at him, I have no idea what he's thinking.

"What?"

"I was afraid that night when you were here for dinner that Ryle would get the wrong idea."

"What do you mean?"

"That he would think it meant you would always be here."

"I won't do that to you." Truman shakes his head. "I don't want to crowd you, Julie. I just want to see Ryle more."

His words jab me like a punch in the belly.

"Stop talking," I whisper. I feel him staring at me, but I take a few seconds to compose myself before looking back at him. "Ryle never said a word about it. But it bothered me."

"That I was here?"

"That you were here." I nod. "And that you never came back for dinner. That we had a nice night, that we almost felt like a family, and then you told me you wanted me to find someone to make me happy."

"Can I talk?" he asks quietly and goes on when I nod, "I want you to be happy. Why is that a bad thing?"

"Which is it, Truman? You want me to be happy with someone else? Or you don't?"

Truman scoots his chair back and stands.

"Are you trying to tell me that you do have feelings for Jerad?"

I sigh and cover my face with my hands. "No, Truman. I'm not."

"Then why are you going to Florida with him?"

I stand, but my knees tremble.

"I'm not. Can we forget about the Florida thing for a minute?"

Truman's face is a mask of confusion, but he nods.

"I'm trying to tell you I'm not gonna move on. I'm not gonna be happy with someone else."

"Jules—" He stands, like he needs to be on his feet to argue.

"I still love you, Truman." My voice shakes with my words. "And you're sending me mixed signals, and things aren't gonna work out, and I need you to—"

He closes his fingers around my wrist and pulls me toward him as he steps closer to me. I meet his eyes, as he lifts his other hand to cup my chin. He's going to kiss me. Having him around that night for dinner isn't going to compare to kissing him, to the way it's going to hurt when he walks out.

But I close my eyes when his lips brush mine. It's our first kiss since I told him I was pregnant. I want more, but I'm frozen with fear. Fear that he'll turn around and walk out. Fear that he'll do it again.

We stand close; his breath is warm on my face. He loosens his grip on my wrist, but he doesn't let go. When I open my eyes, he's watching me. Rather than kiss me again, he smooths his thumb under my chin.

"Julie." He grinds my name out through clenched teeth and still manages to sound hopeful.

I have to end this now, but this is the first time in over six years that we've been this close. I take a minute to remember the curve of his cheek. The scrape of his stubble on my fingers when I touch his face. When I drop my hand and step back, Truman moves with me.

"No." I rest my hand on his chest and shake my head.

"But—"

"It's not that easy, Truman."

"You can't tell me you love me and then change your mind like that."

My eyes fill, but I make myself take another step backwards.

"I think you should go."

"Can't we talk about this?"

Maybe we should talk about this, but no amount of talking is going to make me believe he loves me.

"Not now." I shake my head. "Not with Ryle here."

"But—? Can we?"

"Goodnight, Truman."

CHAPTER SIXTEEN

TRUMAN

She still loves me.

I take that knowledge home the night she tells me, and I wake up with it and carry it around everywhere I go. The trouble is, the words are in my head, not my heart. Not yet. Because she's not happy. It pained her to tell me—to confess to me—that she still loves me. She didn't want to talk about it with Ryle around. She argued that it didn't make anything easy, so I spend the next several days a mix of emotion that makes me act like a moody teenager.

I want her to love me, but I want her to want to love me. I want us to be together, not living apart and making each other miserable. I don't know what to do about it. Of course, my first instinct is to show up at her house again and insist that we talk. But I know better. It wouldn't go well. Even if we got Ryle out of the house for a day, it wouldn't be a good idea to push myself back into Julie's life.

And then there's the whole thing about her going to Florida. First of all, even if it was just she and Dani going, I would dread it. I hate being away from Basset, because I miss time spent with Ryle and Julie. I can't imagine being here with Ryle and climbing the walls missing Julie. Thinking about her kicked back on the beach with a drink. Watching the waves rolls in. Walking in the water and laughing when the waves touch her knees and maybe higher.

Not to mention the possibility that Jerad would go with them. Maybe Julie doesn't have feelings for him, but that doesn't make a beach vacation where they'll be around each other any easier for me to swallow.

Twain and Mabry come to Ryle's next ball game. Ryle's thrilled to see them. Me? Not so much. Since Twain and Harper cornered me on Mom's birthday, I'm angry with both of them. Mostly just because it forced me to say out loud the awful things I said to Jules when we broke up. I'm not proud of that guy, and I feel worse since my siblings know what I did.

I feel like it might have been better to cheat than to suggest she have an abortion since *I* wasn't ready to be a *dad*. Especially with how her dad has treated her all her life.

Dani and Eric sit with Julie—thankfully, the fourth wheel isn't around. I shouldn't be this upset about him, but it makes no sense to me. Like she wants to make me jealous. Except that's not who Julie is. Maybe it's Dani. Either Dani wants to make me see the wonderful woman I lost, or Dani wants Julie to find someone else.

I guess I can't blame her for wanting her best friend to be happy. But her meddling isn't any better than Harper's.

"That poor kid looks just like you," Twain announces. We're standing behind the bleachers, leaning our elbows on the top one. Mabry said hi, but she found Julie and quickly made her way over to sit with her. I watched for a minute as Julie introduced her to her friends, but the whole scene just kind of stuck in my gut and gave me indigestion, so now I'm back to watching the field.

Ryle's on first base tonight.

And he does look just like me.

"Lucky kid, you mean."

Twain snorts.

"Hopefully, if you and Mabry have kids, they'll look like her."

"I'll agree with that." Twain nods, eyes still on the field. "Look at Ethan."

I find Ethan in the third base area, but he's on his knees digging in the dirt.

"Good thing Harp's not here for that."

Keith is here, and I notice he's watching Ethan, but he's much more likely to let Ethan's inattention go than Harper is. She's a stickler for rules and learning.

"You gonna do it?" I nudge Twain's elbow with mine. He turns his head to look at me, the bill of his cap pulled low over his eyes.

"Do what?"

"Marriage and kids and stuff. With Mabry."

"I'd like to," he answers simply. "We'll see."

He turns back to the game, but I stare at him for a moment wondering how he can be so laid back. Harper and I are both so high strung; it's like Twain is adopted or something. I used to think that was a fault, that he wasn't driven like Harper and me. Now I envy it. In my professional and personal life.

"What?" he snaps when he realizes I'm still looking at him.

I shake my head and look away, reminding myself I don't want to talk to either of my siblings about Julie.

"I kissed her the other night."

Way to go, mouth.

I hold my breath waiting for Twain to swoop in and hammer at me with words of wisdom. But he only shoots me a little grin and a lazy shrug.

"She slap you?"

"No."

"Okay, that's a good start."

That's all he says before he focuses on the boys again. I'm shocked and relieved, too, that my mouth decided to tell Twain that and not Harper. If this were Harper, she might grab Julie off the bleachers, drag her back here, and force some sort of confrontation.

When the game's over, the boys run straight to Mabry, stars in their eyes, excited to see her. I get it; she's pretty, and she's fun. She'll be a good aunt. As laid back as Twain is, I do see the two of them tying the knot eventually. I've never seen him happier, and that's saying a lot, because Twain's a positive person.

All of us are standing at the side of the bleachers now, waiting for the boys so we can go home. Mabry tugs on both of their hats, her affection for them lights up her smile. Aunt? She's going to be a good mom one day. That thought makes me happy, but it also turns all of my attention back to Julie.

I wonder if she has her car here, or if she came with Dani and Eric.

"Can we go get ice cream?" Ethan says to Twain. Keith shoots me a deadpan look and rolls his eyes.

"You bet." Twain nods and slaps Ethan's hand in a high five. Ryle shifts his snack to his left hand so he can high five his uncle, too.

"Can I go, Mom?"

Julie glances at me and looks back at Ryle.

"Yes."

The boys throw their fists in the air and holler like they just won the World Series. The smile on Ryle's face warms my heart. He's finally coming out of his shell and becoming more social. I'm glad I'm here to see it.

"I'll bring him home later," Mabry tells Julie.

"Thanks."

Ryle gives me a quick one-armed hug around my legs, and then I spin and watch the boys run to Twain's truck. Twain and Mabry follow hand in hand.

"Gonna go check on Harp," Keith announces, and suddenly, it's just me and Julie and her friends. Dani sizes me up and glances at Julie.

"Wanna grab something to eat?"

Is it my imagination, or does she sound hopeful? Like she wants to get Julie away from me?

"Um." Julie looks at me. I clench my teeth together to keep my traitorous mouth from opening again. Better to play this cool, I remind myself. Let Julie be in charge. "No. I'm good. Thanks."

Dani shoots me a frown, but she nods quickly and flashes me a quick smile.

"Good to see you, Truman," she says as she and Eric head off toward the parking lot.

I consider telling Julie goodbye. Walking away just to see what she would do. But I'm an adult. I don't want to play games. I want this woman back in my life.

"Do you wanna get dinner with me?" I tip my head and hold my breath waiting for her to answer.

She studies my face for a few seconds and finally nods.

"Yeah. I'd like that."

CHAPTER SEVENTEEN

JULIE

Truman surprises me when he suggests we grab sandwiches and go to the park. But I like the idea—after what happened at my house the last time I saw him, I don't trust myself to be alone with him. In the park, we may not be surrounded by people, but we don't have total privacy, either. Not that I plan on jumping him, but even that one kiss was dangerous.

And addictive.

We sit on opposite sides of a picnic table out under a tree. There's no one in the shelter house behind us, but it just feels nice to be out in the open. It's hot, but a gentle breeze keeps it from being sticky.

"Remember playing Frisbee golf with Kent and Leanne?"

Our eyes meet as he asks. I have a mouthful, so I can only nod and smile. Kent was Truman's roommate in college, and Leanne was his girlfriend. We used to hang out with them a lot. The last I heard Kent was working on an oil rig somewhere, and Leanne had moved to British Columbia.

"I put every throw in the trees," I say when I finally swallow.

"Even when we were on an open fairway, you managed to find trees."

His grin is a knife in my heart.

Why wasn't I enough for him? I mean, when he first told me he didn't want the baby, I thought it was because he didn't want to be tied down with the responsibility of a baby. But he eventually came around. Started spending time with Ryle. He traveled a lot even then, but when he was home, he wanted to be with Ryle.

But he never fought to get me back.

"You should take Ryle out to play."

Truman wolfs down another bite of his sub and nods as he chews. "That's a good idea."

"He'd love it."

Truman swallows and looks down at his sandwich. He looks like he's hung up on some deep, heavy thoughts.

"Maybe the three of us could go," he suggests, careful not to meet my eyes.

I open my mouth to say no. To tell him it's not a good idea. But when he looks up at me, I clamp my teeth together and look away.

"You know." I take a sip of my tea and watch a squirrel

climb the tree we're under. "When...when you didn't want Ryle..."

I feel a pang of guilt when I hear his soft groan.

"Jules."

"I worried..." I clear my throat and peek at him, but I look away quickly. Eyes on the flaking green paint on the table, I keep going. "Worried you would be like my dad."

He's watching me with glassy eyes when I look up at him.

"That you would just...pretend like he didn't exist."

"Julie—"

"Just jet set all over the globe and forget he was here."

"I'm not that guy."

I nod, but I can't help the uncertain shrug. "How was I supposed to know that?"

"We were together for a long time," he reminds me. "You should have known me better than that."

"And yet, your suggestion that I have an abortion blew me away."

I see him cringe when I say the word.

"How was I supposed to know?"

"I have never regretted something so much in my life."

"I was crushed." I lick my lips. "For him. Thinking he would grow up without a dad. I mean, wasn't like I knew anything different. He was in my house but never in my life."

Truman stares at me silently, his throat working to hold in emotion.

"But I saw the way your dad was with all of you." My eyes burn with tears. "And when I did the test, and it was positive..."

"What?" he whispers.

"I was scared," I admit. "Scared of being a mom. Of being pregnant. Of giving birth."

We sit in silence for a moment.

"I was scared to tell you. I thought you would be angry. Surprised. But it never occurred to me that you just wouldn't want him. Especially not since we had our future mapped out by that time."

Truman blows out a deep breath. "I'm sorry."

I nod. "I know."

"I had no idea then what being a dad meant. I didn't get that he would be so real, so important, so irreplaceable even in the beginning when you were pregnant."

Not hungry anymore, I fold up the last of my sandwich in the wrapper and tuck it in the bag.

"I thought we could just move on, and we could have another baby someday."

The words are so harsh, so unlike the man I loved—still love —that I close my eyes.

"I didn't get it, Julie." His words are jagged and breathless. "I didn't get how incredible *that* baby would be. I didn't think about him as Ryle. I didn't think about him as a newborn. About his voice saying *Daddy*. I didn't think about him in a ball glove, playing first base."

I nod, because I know he's being honest, and part of me gets it.

"So, we split up, and we moved on," I remind him.

"Did we?" He reaches over the table and strokes his fingers over the back of my hand.

"We've both been with other people now—"

"And that means we can't figure this out?"

"You never fought for me."

"What?" He sounds angry now.

"You came back for him," I say quietly. "But not me."

He groans again and plops his elbows on the table. Muttering under his breath, he shoves his fingers back through his hair and closes his eyes.

"You're a great dad, Truman." I dab at my eyes, frustrated that I'm crying. "You're every bit the dad I thought you could be."

Now he pinches the bridge of his nose and *squeezes* his eyes shut tight.

"You banned me from your life."

"I never—"

"You did." He opens his eyes and stares at me with heat and passion. "You banned me from your life. Yes, you let me spend time with Ryle, but you moved on without me."

"You hurt me," I wail and then ashamed of the way I'm lashing out at him, I put my hand over my mouth and stare at the table. Tears blur the green painted wood now. "What was I supposed to do? You hurt me, Truman."

"I know." He nods and looks away.

"You hurt me in the most intimate way you could," I add. "And you never said you were sorry. And you never came back to fight for me."

Truman sighs and rubs his hands down over his face.

"I thought you were better off without me," he mumbles. "You were too good for me. You—"

"Don't." I shake my head.

"Don't what?"

"Don't make this worse with silly excuses."

"I'm not making excuses," he argues. "Yes, I should have said I was sorry. But I know what I did, the things I said—I know, Julie, what I did to you. I know I disappointed you. I know you didn't trust me with Ryle at first—"

"That's not true."

"It is," he says quietly. "I get it. And yes, eventually, you learned you could trust me. That I wasn't an idiot with a baby. I wasn't taking him and shoving him off on my parents or Harper so I wouldn't have to deal with him."

I did wonder at first if he would do that, but I realized quickly that Truman loved our son and wouldn't hurt him.

"I've had countless hours of therapy to learn that it's not that you don't trust me with him now. It's that you're overprotective, and I know that because I am, too. Because it's part of being a parent. And I know that my feelings of inadequacy when it comes to Ryle are because of the guilt I still have for what I said when you told me you were pregnant."

Stunned that he feels inadequate with Ryle, that he's done therapy, I stare at him silently.

"You went to therapy?"

He flinches. Is he embarrassed to admit that to me?

"Yeah. I did." He takes a deep breath. "We've both had other people in our lives, Jules, but you're it for me. If I can't be with you, I don't wanna be with anyone."

Another knife prick in my heart. I wince and look away.

He hasn't said he loves me. It makes a difference.

"That's what I keep trying to tell Dani." I breathe deeply and feel my nostrils flare. My face is wet and sticky with tears.

"What?" He eyes me curiously.

"I've got Ryle," I answer simply. "I lost the love of my life, but I've got Ryle."

CHAPTER EIGHTEEN

Truman

Jules lets me walk her to her car when we leave, but there's no kiss. Once she's in her car and drives away with a small wave in my direction, I slump against the hood of my car and think about the fact that there was no kiss. But she looked at my lips before she turned around and pulled her door open to get in.

While I would have rather kissed her, knowing that she was thinking about it makes me feel a little lighter when I finally get in my car. We're circling each other in a holding pattern, but things have changed somewhat, because we cleared the air. I hate knowing that I hurt her, that she thought I was willing to just walk away from her and never look back. But on the other hand, it's good to know what she's thinking.

In fact, the next weeks are easier for me to get through. It's like Julie's a happy place in my head again. It's not quite like it was when we were together, obviously, but the hope that we find our way back to each other makes me lighthearted.

Now when I go to Ryle's games, I make sure to sit by her—even if Dani and Eric are with her. I don't crowd her. I know pushing my way back into her life isn't the answer.

But now I know how important it is that she knows I want to be with her. I want to be a family with her and Ryle.

She's around more now. I suppose I have Harper to thank for that. Seems like every time I go to my sister's these days, Julie's there. Harper might be inviting her over, encouraging her to hang around, but when they're not looking at me watching them, I see their friendship growing. With Mabry, too.

As much as I appreciate Harper for befriending Julie again, in our adulthood, I still feel weird talking to her—after the big reveal of the crappy thing I did to Julie and Ryle. It's not like I can just bury it again, not with Harper apparently orchestrating this opportunity for me and Julie to reconnect. I guess I'll just hold my breath and hope that Harper keeps it to herself—not something I care to discuss with my mom. And that maybe if Julie and I would ever reconcile, Harper might bury it for me, and we'd never discuss it again.

"Hey."

Julie's shiny glossed lips tip up in a smile when she opens the door to me. I'm here to pick Ryle up. He doesn't know it yet, but we're going to play Frisbee golf.

"He's finishing his lunch," she tells me and nods for me to come inside.

Ryle waves at me with a mouthful of what I'm guessing is grilled cheese, based on the torn edges of crust on his plate.

"Are you ready for an adventure?" I join him at the table.

"Yep." He nods, takes a gulp of milk, and puts his glass back down.

"Finish your vegetables," Julie reminds him as she grabs the skillet off the burner and slips it in the sink. Ryle looks at me as he picks up a carrot stick. I can't help but laugh out loud when he rolls his eyes. Julie turns from the sink and eyes me suspiciously. "What?"

I shake my head, but from the corner of my eye, I see Ryle grinning.

He climbs off his chair when he shoves the last bite in his mouth, hands his plate to Julie, and hurries out of the room. I watch him go, but when we're alone, I look back at Julie. She's wearing a yellow sundress and simple flat sandals. With her hair pulled back in a loose ponytail, she looks eighteen—carefree and happy.

"What're you doing while we're gone?"

She must have a date. And though I suspect I would feel the same pit in my stomach no matter who it's with, I hold my breath, assuming she'll say Jerad.

"Nothing." She shrugs. "Thought about updating Ryle's scrapbook."

"You still do that?"

When Ryle was a baby, she made detailed scrapbooks and shared them with my mom. She gave me one, but mostly, she gives me small photo albums. I didn't realize she still did the whole scrapbooking thing.

"Not like I used to," she admits. She stands with her back to me, hands in the soapy water, washing the skillet.

"You look awfully pretty to sit by yourself and scrapbook."

She looks up at me when I join her at the sink. Her cheeks are tinged with pink, but she offers me a tiny smile.

"I had coffee with Mabry this morning."

I feel my whole body relax. I know she keeps telling me she's not interested in anyone else, but the more I see her, the more we talk now, the more aware I am of how badly it would hurt to watch her fall for someone else.

"That sounds fun."

She nods as she works, turning her attention back to the skillet. "Yeah. I like her. She's a perfect match for Twain."

"So." I take a deep breath and decide to go for it. "Wanna go with me and Ryle today?"

She doesn't flat out tell me no. Instead, she tips her head back to look at me for a moment. "What're you guys going to do?"

"Thought we'd try a few holes of Frisbee golf."

A laugh slips from her lips, and she shakes her head.

"No?"

"You want me to teach him how to find trees?"

"Maybe how not to throw a Frisbee."

"Wow." She nods, and this time, she laughs out loud.

"Wanna go?"

Our eyes meet again and finally, she nods. "Yeah. I'll go."

Rather than throwing my arms around her and gathering her in close like I want to, I stand my ground and lean in to kiss her. Just a soft press of my lips on hers.

"You gotta quit doing that, Truman," she whispers as she turns back to the sink.

"Why?"

"What if Ryle sees us kissing?"

"We weren't kissing."

"What?" She tips her head and shoots me a frown.

"That was just a peck." I turn sideways at the sink and study her face. "This is kissing."

She meets me halfway this time. Her lips are warm and wet against mine, and she rests her hand on my forearm. Her fingers are warm and sudsy. She tastes like coffee, and she smells like sunshine and school and backpacks and hot chocolate at Friday night football games.

"I don't want to rush into something, Truman." She ends the kiss, but she doesn't back away. I can't help but touch her when she rests her forehead on my chest. I press the tips of my fingers to the back of her neck. Her ponytail slides over the back of my hand.

"We're six years behind, Jules," I remind her.

She pats my chest and steps back when we hear Ryle coming down the hall to the kitchen. He climbs back on his chair, rests his elbows on the table, and props his chin in his hands.

"I'm ready."

"Mom's gonna go with us," I tell him. The words chase a little thrill through me. Maybe it's a mistake to rush this, but I can't hold back how I feel. I've waited six years to say that to my son, to say that his mom's going to do something with us. It has a nice ring to it.

Ryle nods, but he doesn't seem overly impressed. Julie and I glance at each other. She seems relieved. I guess she's right. Making sure we don't hurt Ryle is the top priority. It's okay if he doesn't see the three of us doing something together as a momentous event. This time, we'll save the hoping and finger crossing to the adults.

CHAPTER NINETEEN

JULIE

My Frisbee throwing skills haven't improved much at all, but I'm okay with that. Ryle is having the time of his life—not just with the Frisbee and Truman, but the two of them are doubled-over in laughing fits every few minutes. Sometimes at me, and others I have no idea what's funny. But I love seeing the two of them having fun together.

There could be more of this.

The thought is pinging around inside me the whole time we're playing. Whether we rush into something or not, Truman seems to be telling me he wants to be a family. He wouldn't push this if he didn't want to be around me and Ryle both. I know that.

But my heart still wants to hear him say he loves me.

At the end of the Frisbee outing, we get ice cream, and then Ryle wants to drive the go-karts at Twain's place. Truman asks me if I care. When I agree to go, Ryle does his new move—throwing a celebratory fist in the air.

I wonder if Truman's family knows something might be going on between us now. I wonder if Harper set out to make something happen between us. I guess I don't mind the push, whatever it took to nudge Truman in my direction again.

Ryle seems slightly disappointed when we get to the go-kart track and Ethan isn't there. I want to remind him that Ethan doesn't live here, but then Twain grabs him and throws him over his shoulder in a fireman's carry and Ryle's giggling, delighted to have his uncle's attention.

Twain gets in a go-kart with Ryle, and so I go out on the track and claim one for myself. When I look back, Truman is at the gate by the attendant, mouth agape watching me.

"Let's go, Woolff," I call him out, and he accepts my challenge with a grin.

First I pay more attention to Twain and Ryle, but finally, my competitive streak kicks in. Ryle's having a blast, so I start watching Truman's go-kart, and I do my best to lap him.

Later, Truman carries Ryle inside. Since he conked out in the car on the way home, I tell Truman to take him straight to his bedroom, and we wrestle him into his pajamas without waking him.

It's been such a good day I don't want it to end. But I'm a little fidgety as Truman and I make our way back down the hall to the living area of the house. Whether we rush back together or not, I'm not ready to take anything further physically. And not just because Ryle's in the house.

"Thank you," Truman says softly. I follow him when he goes straight to the door. I'm a bit relieved and a bit disappointed that he knows sticking around right now isn't a good idea.

"For what?" I fold my arms over my chest and tip my head at him. "Being your comic relief?"

His grin is the same as it was eight, even ten years ago, and I have to jerk my gaze away from his face.

"Well, that too."

"Thanks for asking me to go," I tell him.

He shoves his hands into his hip pockets, and I recognize the move. He's reminding himself we're not there yet. Too soon to dive headfirst into anything. Best to tiptoe back to the physical relationship we used to have. It's the same reason I'm standing here with my arms over my chest. I need the barrier, because part of me would love to throw my arms around Truman and never let go.

"So." He clears his throat. "Still going to Florida?"

"Yeah." I nod. "Just Dani and me."

He groans softly. "I love that you're gonna get a little break and soak up some beach time." I know him well enough to know he's sincere. "But I hate that you're gonna be gone. Especially now."

I do, too, but I refuse to have second thoughts on hanging out with my best friend. And being apart right now might be good for both of us. It's a natural brake for how quickly things are moving right now. Maybe if I'm gone for a few days, Truman will remember he doesn't need me. Doesn't love me. That we'd be better off as friends raising our son together.

The thought makes me queasy.

Maybe being away from each other will make everything a little easier to see, too. Maybe we'll miss each other in a different way than we've been missing each other for the past six years.

"I know." I nod. "But I'm looking forward to it."

"You should be," he agrees with me. "When do you leave?"

"Thursday."

"Five days."

"Yeah."

"And you'll be gone how long?" he asks me.

"Back on Monday afternoon."

"And it's okay with you if I see Ryle? Every day?"

"Of course it is," I answer immediately. "I want that for both of you, Truman."

"One more question."

I laugh and nod for him to ask away.

"I don't wanna bother you on your getaway, but...can we text at all?"

"I'd like that."

Truman whooshes out a deep breath. I watch him draw his hands from his pockets and wrap one around the back of his neck.

"Good." He raises his eyebrows. "Guess I should get going."

"I'll see you Tuesday night?"

Tuesday is our snack night for Ryle's baseball team.

"Yes." He nods. "But can we not take carrot sticks?"

"What?"

His question makes me laugh.

"Can we be the fun parents? Take some fruit snacks?"

Me and Truman. The fun parents. I like the sound of that.

"What if we did fruit snacks and juice boxes?"

"See? That's awesome."

He reaches behind him to open the door. Afraid he's going to leave without kissing me goodbye, I grab for his arm and lean in to kiss him.

"I thought maybe another kiss would be pushing my luck."

"Goodnight, Truman." I kiss his lips again, brush a kiss on his cheek, and step back.

Obviously, it's not an issue now, but as I get ready for bed, I decide that at some point we're going to have to talk about the future. If we get back together, will we have more children? I'd love that. But I need to know that Truman's on board this time for everything.

I can't watch him walk away again.

CHAPTER TWENTY

TRUMAN

When Julie calls me Tuesday evening before Ryle's ballgame, I'm at the office about ready to knock off for the night. I've just rearranged my travel schedule for the next ten days, so I can be home with Ryle from now until after Julie comes back from her beach trip with Dani. I shut my computer down, mind racing with all the things Ryle and I can do, including more Frisbee golf, but so much more comes to mind. My dad spent a lot of time with us when we were kids, and I've been remembering all the stuff we did with him and wondering if Ryle would be interested in model planes and cars and going swimming and butterfly gardens.

Twain and I were never big on the butterfly gardens; that was more Harper's thing. But I guess it was okay when I was Ryle's age. We did like catching lightning bugs, so maybe Ryle and I can hang out and do that one night.

But the good feelings are gone in a wave of unease when I see Julie's name on my phone. My first thought is worry for Ryle. What if something happened? While things have definitely changed for the better recently between us, Julie and I aren't at the point where we just call each other through the day just to say hi. Maybe I'm overreacting, but my first reaction is panic over Ryle being injured. Then I worry about Julie. What if she's sick or had an accident? After all, I always thought Harper was invincible, and look what happened to her.

But really, even that worry simmers to a low burn quickly, and I'm left with a feeling of dread. What if it's simply that Julie's thought about the things we've said to each other the past few days and changed her mind? What if she's okay with me being around more for Ryle, but she's decided she doesn't want to get involved with me again?

"Hey."

A little wave of relief rolls over me when my voice sounds normal. I'm heading out to my car now, my head already with Ryle at his ball game. Just need to go home and change clothes, and I'll be ready.

"Hey!" Julie sounds excited, which makes me feel a little bit better. She wouldn't call me to say she changed her mind about us and sound like that, would she?

"What's goin' on?"

"Have you left work? Are you busy?"

"Leaving now," I answer as I aim my fob at my car. "What's up?"

"Um." I hear it in her soft laugh. She's nervous. "I just thought we could go together to get the snack for tonight. You know, since we wanna be the cool parents and bring something fun."

She's asking me to go with her to the store. I slump into the driver's seat, so relieved I'm speechless for a moment.

"I mean, if you don't have time, it's fine," she rushes in when I don't say anything. "Ryle and I can pick something out. I just thought you and Ryle—"

"I'll go!" I interrupt her. "I can go with you guys."

Now she's quiet, and I hold my breath, wondering if I was a little too enthusiastic with my answer.

"Okay."

"I thought something was wrong," I admit. I start my car and wait for the call to switch to hands free mode, and then I back out of my parking space slowly. "When I saw your name come up."

"Oh." She groans softly. "I'm sorry. I guess I don't call you too often."

She never calls me, but I don't point that out to her.

"Let me run home and change clothes. Then I'll come by and get you guys. Does that work?"

"Absolutely! Hey, Ryle's eating his dinner. Do you want me to fix you a plate?"

"Sure. Thank you."

"See you in a few."

After I end the call, it still takes the rest of the drive for my heart rate to slow down to normal. Makes me wonder how bad Julie felt when I called her from the hospital. I tune into the drive, paying attention as I cross the city streets to my apartment. It's an okay place, and normally, I like spending time here. But knowing Julie and Ryle are waiting for me at her place makes me rush inside and change my clothes as fast as possible without tripping out of my pants and ending up on the floor.

I wonder what Ryle will pick for a snack. I can think of a lot of things that sound good, but this is Ryle's choice. I know he likes cookies, but will he choose those for a snack for his team? It hits me that it's kind of sad that he's my son, and I don't know him well enough to know what his go-to junk food is.

Ryle's sliding away from the table when Julie lets me in. He flashes me a grin and disappears down the hall. I assume he's washing his hands and getting ready to leave. Julie wears a cute smile when she hands me a plate.

"Dinosaur chicken nuggets." I laugh and nod. "Okay. Sounds good."

"Ryle thought you would be really excited," she agrees.

"And mac and cheese." I scoop a bite of the noodles and look at Julie when I stick the fork in my mouth. "And I'm guessing the peas were your choice."

"What is it with you and vegetables?" She rolls her eyes. "Are you this picky when you're traveling? Do you ask the waiters at Michelin restaurants to hold the haricots verts?"

"Of course not," I answer with a mouthful. "I like green beans."

She shakes her head like she's frustrated, but her smile is too sincere for me to believe it for a second.

I scarf the dinner down, secretly thrilled that she made me a plate, even if I am eating six-year-old fare. It's good, too, because I skipped lunch. Too busy with rearranging my schedule to stop and eat.

Ryle appears in the kitchen as I stick the last bite of a chicken nugget in my mouth. He's dressed for his ball game, complete with his glove. I carry my plate to the sink and rinse it, but Julie snatches it from me and washes it quickly.

"We ready?" she asks when she dries it and puts it away.

"Dad, I'm gonna hit a home run tonight," Ryle announces.

"Sounds awesome."

"Let's go, guys," Julie says as she picks up her purse. "Gotta stop at the store so we can get your snack, Ryle."

"Rocket pops!" he yells, fists in the air, as we head out the door. Julie and I exchange a smile as we follow him to my car.

"Not sure they'll stay frozen, Ry," Julie says quietly.

"We can get a Styrofoam cooler," I tell her. "And ice."

We stare at each other over the car. Ryle, who had started to climb in, leans out and grabs onto Julie's forearm.

"Can we, Mom?"

She blinks at me, and the corners of her mouth turn up just a tiny bit. When she looks at Ryle, though, the smile grows.

"Sure."

CHAPTER TWENTY-ONE

JULIE

Eric drops Dani off at the game. He's meeting Jerad at some apartment complex. I guess Jerad really is thinking about moving here. Thankfully, Dani finally quit trying to push me at him. We've hung out a little bit this summer—the four of us. I've made it clear I have no interest in dating him. I'm nervous about tonight, though. About Dani sitting so close to me on one side, and Truman and his family on the other side. I mean, Truman and I aren't hanging on each other. In fact, there's at least a foot between us on the bleacher, but we're talking and laughing together, and his family is talking to me like I'm part of them.

Dani notices. Of course she does. She catches my eye a time or two or ten and raises her eyebrows as if to ask what's going on, if I'm okay. Beyond telling her that Truman and I have been talking more lately, I haven't said much about it. Whatever Truman and I are doing feels special, and it's all new again, and that makes it fragile to me. I'm not ready to share it with anyone, not even Dani.

Instead, every time she catches my eye, I smile to let her know it's okay. *I'm okay.*

Ryle does get a nice hit, though it's not exactly a home run. His coach helps him stretch the hit into extra bases, and he sends him home even though the pitcher is holding the ball. The lefty on the mound makes a play on Ryle at the plate, and naturally, my kid slides dramatically and comes up with at least half the dirt on the infield on his pants. He throws his fists in the air, and his buddies slap him on the back.

It's painfully adorable, because it takes me back to Truman's high school baseball days, and our son looks just like his dad. And because it gives me a vision of what my kid's going to be like when he's older. For a minute, time flies, and I'm sad about losing my son.

"Hey." Truman bumps my arm with his. "What's wrong?"

I meet his eyes and laugh softly. "I just had a flash of Ryle playing varsity ball like you."

Truman's smile is like a warm, solid hug on a cold winter day.

"We're gonna blink, and this is all gonna be over."

Truman acknowledges the truth in what I said with a small nod. "But. Hopefully when we get there, we'll still have each other."

His quiet words are like an arrow—Cupid's stupid arrow—in my heart.

"Do you think so?"

"And…" He leans in close to me and whispers so only I can hear him. "We could have more babies."

Floored by what he said, at the thought of Truman and I making a future together, having more children together, the implication of that—of being with Truman that way again—I stare at him in stunned silence. Dani leans close on the other side to say something, and I feel heat rise in my cheeks.

Truman tips his head to study my face. I glance at Dani and then look back at him.

"No?"

He hasn't said he loves me. But maybe he does. Maybe if he's talking about being together when Ryle gets older, if he's talking about having more kids, maybe he does love me. My heart is pounding in my throat, and I'm hyperaware of Dani watching us now. Rather than answer Truman with words, I reach for his hand and link our fingers together. Truman holds on, even when Dani makes a show of looking.

Ethan catches a pretty nasty-looking fly ball on second. It's a high one—Twain calls it a tall can of corn—and it looks wicked, like it's got some spin on it. Maybe the batter hit it off the end of the bat. Ethan looked equal parts thrilled and surprised to catch it. When their team comes off the field after the final batter, Ethan looks at us on the bleachers and flashes us a thumbs up.

"Wish we would have recorded that," Harper says with a groan.

"I did!" Lilian leans forward and rests her hand on Harper's shoulder. Still in the cast, Harper is on the bottom bleacher. She turns with a smile to thank her mom, but her eyes stop on me and Truman. On our intwined fingers.

I don't know why but I hold my breath. Harper and I have talked more this summer than we ever did before. She's been at my house a few times, enough to stir things up between me and Truman. She meets my eyes and smiles, and I know then she said the things she did on purpose. Maybe Truman talks to her about us. Maybe she had a hunch. Whatever the case, she meddled, but at the moment, I'm kind of glad she did.

The rocket pops on ice are a hit after the game. They're still frozen. The boys are thrilled. And it's hot enough outside that the parents don't say a word about the cold, sugary treat. I stand at the end of the bleachers watching the boys gather around Ryle, all of them talking to him and at him all at once. I'm not sure I've ever seen him this happy. It wasn't that long ago that Ryle was a very quiet boy.

"Where'd ya get these?" One little boy asks Ryle.

"You can get 'em about anywhere," Ryle announces. His nonchalance tickles me. "But my mom and dad got 'em for me."

My heart is so full at the moment it hurts.

For the first time in my son's life, Truman and I did something together for and with him. It should have always been like this, but now's not the time for regrets. It's time to look ahead and dream about what the three of us can do together.

As much as I'm looking forward to getting away with Dani and lounging on the beach, part of me wants to stay here with Ryle. And Truman. Doing other things that families do together.

CHAPTER TWENTY-TWO

Truman

"Why did Mom have to go to Florida?"

Ryle spent last night at my place. I cleared it with Julie, though honestly, that was a little weird. We keep saying we're going to take things slowly, but in reality, things are moving faster. Shopping with her and Ryle the other night was awesome. I'm painfully aware that most guys my age might roll their eyes at me as they head out for a night at the club. But I don't care. Holding hands with Jules at Ryle's ballgame—not pulling away when someone noticed—made me feel ten feet tall. Julie's letting people see that she's mine. That we belong together.

So, yeah, after all of that, it felt weird to ask her again if it's okay if Ryle's with me when she's gone. I think she thought so, too. It's not like I'm going to demand that he stay with me the entire time she's gone. I know he's excited about spending time at Harper's, so he and Ethan can hang out.

Yes, my six-year-old informed me they don't play; they hang out.

"She didn't have to," I answer.

Ryle scoops a bite of cereal, but he keeps his eyes on me. I offered to make him pancakes and bacon, but he asked for Kix cereal. And then rattled off the lines from the commercial, promising me that Julie wouldn't care if he ate it.

"But you have to? When you leave, you have to go?" He finally puts the spoon in his mouth. His words leave me rattled, like a sucker punch. "For work?"

"Well, yeah, but I haven't been doing as much of that," I remind him. I don't want a pat on the back. That's not why I've tried to slow down my traveling, but I hope Ryle at least realizes I've been home a lot more often lately.

"I know." He nods as he chews. "I like when you're here."

Our eyes lock for a second, and I feel a little thrill roll through me. I take a bite of my cereal and wonder why he chose Kix. I mean, if I were a kid and my mom was gone for a few days, I'd ask for all the sugary stuff she never lets me have.

"So, why did Mom go?"

"Do you miss her?"

Is he going to have a meltdown after only one night of Julie being gone? She and Dani left for the airport yesterday afternoon. I picked Ryle up at her place, so I saw her smother him with goofy smiles and kisses. Ryle hugged her and clung hard to her—they're not apart very often. But he didn't seem upset when she left. And I thought we did okay last night. We grilled chicken; I let him help me flip it once, so he felt like he contributed. We ate at the kitchen island, debating the best superhero for dinner conversation. I say Iron Man, but Ryle likes the Hulk. He also informed me that Julie likes Thor—big surprise, right?

After dinner, we watched *SpiderMan*. And then we read a *Scooby Doo* book—I read most of it, but Ryle read a few paragraphs to me.

Ryle shrugs in answer to my question. "Kinda. But you let me stay up later than she does."

I laugh, relieved he didn't say he misses her and that he's miserable and wants to go home.

"Mom went to hang out on the beach with Dani."

"Mom says Dani's going to have a baby."

"She is," I answer with a nod. We're both still eating; Ryle slurps his spoonfuls, and somehow he's got a milk mustache now. Not sure how he managed that; he's drinking orange juice. "That's why they went."

"She's gonna have the baby there?" He screws his face up into a frown, and I remind myself I'm talking to a six-year-old. I need to be more direct when I talk.

"No. But when Dani does have her baby, she'll be tired. Babies don't sleep a lot. Or as well as we do. They wake up in the night and cry."

"Cuz they poop their diapers."

I stare at my son for a moment and try not to laugh.

"Well, yeah, they do. And they get hungry. So Dani will be up with her baby a lot. She wanted to relax on the beach."

"Is Mom having a baby, too?" Ryle tips his head. "Is that why she went?"

This time, Ryle's words are a knife in my heart. Because I missed it the first time Julie was pregnant. I missed feeling Ryle move in her belly. Missed any crazy cravings she might have had. Missed watching her deliver my baby into this world. I hope she'll be pregnant again one day soon. With my baby. But I can't say that to Ryle.

"No. She's just going for some relaxation. Mom works hard. She gets a break, too."

"I like the beach."

"You've never been to the beach." I ruffle his hair as I stand and carry my empty bowl to the dishwasher.

"But I would like it."

"You might." I nod. "But all moms need breaks. She's probably kicked back on a towel, snoozing."

In a swimsuit. Maybe a bikini. That thought makes my heart pound.

"She's probably building sandcastles."

Doubtful, but now I wonder if it's not that Ryle misses Julie, but maybe he's jealous that he isn't building sandcastles.

"Maybe, but we're gonna do something even better."

"What's better than sandcastles?" he asks around another mouthful.

"Have you ever flown a plane?"

"I can't even drive a car, Dad." He rolls his eyes, and I have a vision of what he's going to be like when he's ten or twelve.

"Just a sec."

He watches me leave the kitchen, but he doesn't follow me. I need to remember to tell Julie about this conversation when we talk next. She FaceTimed last night from her hotel room, so she could see Ryle. I talked to her for a few minutes; she was in a sleep shirt, sitting up in her bed. Beautiful. I hope she calls again to talk to Ryle. No, I hope she FaceTimes again, so I get to see her again.

I hid the remote control airplane in my closet. Twain and I had remote control cars when we were kids, and we loved them. Well, we loved race cars and Hot Wheels and racetracks, so of course we loved remote control cars. Ryle has one—I got it for him last year for his birthday. He played with it for a while, but I'm hoping to spark some interest with a plane.

I'm banking on it being fun, different, since he and I can take it out together.

"What's that?" he asks when I carry the box into the kitchen. He's at the sink, on his tiptoes, rinsing his bowl out.

"A remote control airplane."

He tips his head and stares at me suspiciously.

"Lemme see it."

"See it? How about we go to the park and fly it?"

"Can we?" His grin lights up his face.

"Of course we can!" I anticipate his fist bump and throw my hand up for it.

"Mom would say I have to brush my teeth first."

"Then you better go brush your teeth," I say with a shrug.

"Are you and Mom getting married?" he asks as he goes down the hall to the bathroom.

His question stuns me. I nearly drop the box. What does he know about marriage? I mean, obviously, he knows his family isn't the same as other kids' families at school. But he can't be the only kid who lives with just his mom. But does he understand what marriage is? Well, no, he can't really understand it, but what does he think it is?

I follow him to the bathroom and prop myself in the doorway. He puts a pea-sized amount of paste on his toothbrush and then leans forward to turn the faucet on. Our eyes meet in the square mirror over the sink. I don't know how to answer him.

"Are you?" he asks again.

I can't say yes. Because we're not there yet. I am. I'm all in. I'd put a tux on tomorrow and meet Julie at St. John's—her parents' church—or City Hall. But we haven't talked that far ahead, and talking about it with Ryle first would be a big mistake.

"I don't know, Ryle." I sigh, my voice gruff with emotion I hope he doesn't pick up on. If Jules and I don't get back together now, after easing back into a new level of whatever it is we're doing, it's going to kill me.

"Do you wanna marry her?" he asks innocently. He sticks the brush in his mouth, but he turns to face me and stares at me pointedly.

"What do you know about marriage?" I ask him. Maybe if he tells me what he's thinking, I'll know better how to handle this. I slip into the room with him and park on the edge of the tub.

"You're in the same house," he answers. "Like Grandpa and Grandma."

"Yeah."

"And she makes you coffee, and you tell her she's pretty."

"I'd like that." The words are out before I can stop them.

"You hafta tell her that every day." He purses his sudsy lips as if he's not sure he could do that in my position.

"Your mom's beautiful, Ryle," I answer truthfully. "I could tell her that every day."

"So, you do wanna marry her." He shrugs.

"There's more to it than that, buddy." I stand and wait while he brushes for a few minutes.

"Like what?" he asks when he rinses.

"Grown up stuff."

"Kissing." He turns his nose up.

"What do you know about that?" I laugh when he looks up at me, his face a mask of horror.

"Aunt Harper and Uncle Keith kiss a lot," he moans and shivers. "So do Uncle Twain and Mabry."

"Gotcha."

When he puts his toothbrush away and dries his hands and mouth, I herd him out the door and back to the kitchen, thinking our conversation is over.

"Do you kiss Mom?"

Wondering how I got stuck in this conversation, wondering how Julie would answer him—if she's ever had to field these kinds of questions—I pick up the airplane box and grab my keys.

"Sometimes."

"What else?" he asks me.

Not sure what he's asking, I aim a frown at him. "What else what?"

"Grown up stuff?"

I nearly swallow my tongue. Seriously? He's six. Do kids know things at that age that we didn't?

"What do you mean?" I stick my keys in my pocket and drop a hand on his shoulder to steer him to the door. The sooner we get to the park and get this plane in the air, the better.

"Do you fight with Mom?"

A little bit relieved, I sigh as I get him settled into his booster seat.

"Sometimes."

"Then you're married." He shrugs.

Seatbelt clicked around him, I draw back and stare at him. He's serious as a heart attack. I have to say something. I can't let him think that, because chances are this will come up later when he's talking to Julie. If she thinks I'm putting ideas in his head, ideas about us getting back together, she'll be angry with me.

And rightly so. As much as I want her back, I wouldn't use our son to do it.

"Nope." I shake my head.

"You kiss, and you fight." He shrugs again. "Like Aunt Harper and Uncle Keith—"

"Mom doesn't make me coffee." I latch onto the one thing he mentioned about his ideas of marriage that Julie doesn't do. I feel a little bit guilty when he sinks back against the seat and sighs.

Glad to have that conversation behind us, I hurry around the car and get in the driver's seat.

"Dad?"

"Hmm?" I meet his eyes in the rearview as I start the car and put it in drive.

"Do you want to marry Mom?"

"Can I ask you something, Ryle?"

"Yep."

I laugh softly and wonder when my kid grew up. I feel like I'm talking to a teenager instead of an incoming first grader.

"Do you want me to marry your mom?"

"Would you live with us then?"

I hold my breath for a second, hoping Julie would understand why I feel compelled to answer him honestly.

"Yes."

"Would you get me a baby brother?"

"I don't know, Ryle. Do you want a baby brother?"

"Yeah." He nods, but he looks away. "Would you be like Grandpa and Grandma?"

Panic shoots through me as I jerk my gaze back to the rearview mirror to look at him. What has he seen my parents doing?

"What do you mean?"

"Would you guys be happy?"

I feel like he knocked the air out of me again. I can only nod, because yes, I would be happy to be married to Julie and living in their house and kissing her.

"Yeah, we would." I have to hope she would say the same thing.

"Then yes." He nods. "I want you to marry Mom."

CHAPTER TWENTY-THREE

JULIE

"So?"

Dani's been patient. We've been gone for an entire day now, and she hasn't asked about Truman. I know she saw us holding hands at Ryle's tee-ball game the other night, so she's got to be bursting with questions. I appreciate her patience, but on the other hand, all afternoon on the beach today, I was tense, just waiting for her to start the interrogation.

I don't mean to sound harsh. After all, Dani was there when Truman left. Dani was my shoulder to cry on. She held my hand when Ryle was born. She sat with him as a newborn when I needed a break. She did my laundry and insisted I nap.

All that without ever knowing why we broke up.

And now she sees her best friend falling into something that might break her heart, so she has every right to demand answers.

"He never cheated," I tell her, rather than launching into what did happen.

She stares at me over the high-top table and rolls her eyes.

"No kidding, Julie." She sighs.

"What does that mean?"

"Well, for one thing, he adored you."

Her words sting. Once upon a time, I thought he did. And then, it felt like I—like my son and I—meant nothing to him. And now, I'm back feeling like I might be special to him. It's a heady feeling, but I'm scared, too.

"Besides," she sips her caffeine-free soda and continues, "You guys loved each other. If he would have cheated, you would have forgiven him."

"You think so?" That surprises me. I'm not sure I would have.

"I do." She nods. "So, whatever happened was bigger. Worse."

"Yeah." I bite my lip, dreading this conversation.

"He didn't want Ryle." She says it point blank and then tacks on, "Did he?"

I hate this. I hate what it does to me, but even more, I hate how it paints Truman. He hurt me, yes. But if I had been different then, if my own father had treated me better—if my own father had *loved* me—maybe I would have reacted differently to Truman's fear of responsibility. Maybe I'm as much to blame for the way things happened as he is.

"No."

"He wanted you to have an abortion."

I nod. "How long have you known that?"

"Since I held your hand when Ryle was born."

My eyes blur with tears.

"You never told me," Dani says softly, "which told me something else."

"What?" I reach for my margarita, wishing for something stronger.

"You were protecting him," she says simply. "From anyone who cared about you. You didn't want anyone to hate him."

"Dani—"

"Because you were still in love with him."

I take another gulp of my drink and stare at her in silence. Of course, she figured things out years ago and stayed quiet. Because she's my best friend, and she knew I loved him. She never sided with him, but she never went on the attack, either.

"Am I stupid?"

"Stupid? No." She pats my hand on the tabletop and offers me a little smile. "But is it time to end this? For you and Ryle and Truman to be a family? Yes."

"You think we should be a family?"

"Yeah." She nods. "I do. You should be living under the same roof. You should be sleeping in his arms every night. And you should be raising that kid together. Not only does Ryle deserve that, Julie, you and Truman do, too."

Most girls probably talk to their mothers about things like this. I talk to my mom about buying new curtains or needing a new dishwasher. She wouldn't have understood the hurt I felt when Truman suggested terminating the pregnancy.

It means something that Dani believes in me and Truman.

"You've never moved on. Not really." She plucks another nacho from the plate and crunches it. She'll have heartburn before we walk out of here; I know, I've been there. But she's craving the chicken and cheese. And I know that feeling, too. "Neither of you."

"We've tried," I remind her.

"But it's never worked." She crunches another nacho. "And maybe that's because you're meant to be together."

"I'm scared, Dani."

"Let me ask you something."

"What?"

"What're you afraid of?"

Before I can open my mouth, she holds up her hand and goes on, "You could live the next six or twelve or twenty years without Truman. Or you could take a risk and love him and marry him and be happy together."

"What if we hurt Ryle?"

"He's a well-adjusted kid. You guys have made sure of that," she says with wide eyes. "I think giving him both parents in a house, a sibling or two...I think it's worth the risk, don't you?"

"Marry him," I repeat her words and blow out a nervous sigh.

"I see the way you look at him," she tells me. "Not just the last week or two. Anytime you're around him. I see it. Eric sees it."

"Okay, there's no question I'm in love with him," I admit. "But I don't know if he feels the same way."

"It's been six years. Seven since you told him you were pregnant." She takes another drink and then presses her fist to her chest. "Ugh. Why are you letting me eat these?"

I laugh softly. "The pregnant mama wants what the pregnant mama wants."

"And the heart wants what the heart wants," she answers, and then she cackles when I roll my eyes. "Why else are you both still alone, Julie? Because you're meant to be together."

I take a deep breath and answer with a small nod.

"So, yes? You're gonna marry him?"

"Whoa! Whoa!" I shake my head and grab my margarita again. "Let's not get carried away. We're hanging out. He's kissed me a few times. No one's said anything about marriage."

"If he asked you tomorrow, would you say yes?"

"No, because I'll be on the beach with you, and I'm not gonna accept a marriage proposal by FaceTime."

"'kay." She grins and rolls her eyes. "I'll give you that one. But my point is, dragging your feet didn't work. You've been dragging your feet through life since Ryle was born. Rush it, Julie. Rush in and grab Truman Woolff and be happy."

"He got Ryle a remote control airplane," I tell her, feeling a little bit giddy now about Truman, the father of my child. Truman—the man I never stopped loving. "They took it to the park to fly it today."

"Very cool."

"I can't wait to talk to Ryle later."

"And Truman."

"Well, yeah, but I wanna hear Ryle tell me about the plane."

"Do you have any Tums?"

"No. You don't?"

"Ran out."

"Then I guess we need to get you to the store to get you some Tums," I say as I finish my drink. I have to fight to stay in my chair and not rush her out of here. Actually, we have two more days here, and now that we've talked about this, about Truman, I want to rush her out of Florida and go home to my guys.

CHAPTER TWENTY-FOUR

TRUMAN

Ryle rattles about the plane long enough that I start to think it's less about the excitement than about trying to stay up past his bedtime again. It's great, though, flopped out on the bed beside him while he FaceTimes Julie and tells her about his day. He watched me fly it for a bit, like he was afraid to try it. It reminded me of the way he used to be so timid and quiet. I'm not sure what brought him out of that; I'd like to think I had some hand in it. That maybe being around him more brought something vital to his confidence. Probably wishful Dad thinking, but whatever.

Julie laughs as she talks to him, and while I listen, I can't help but wish we were a year into the future. Julie and me married. Maybe another baby on the way. Maybe we're talking on FaceTime because she's traveling for work, and I'm being a stay-at-home dad.

"Hey!" she says. "Let me talk to your dad for a minute, Ryle."

That comment feeds right into my fantasies, but I give myself a mental shake as Ryle hands me the iPad and hops off the foot of the bed.

"Where ya going?" I ask him.

"I'm hungry."

I cringe as he hurries out of the room, and I look back at the screen. But Julie's smiling when I look at her.

"You're spoiling him, aren't you?"

"Maybe."

"Sounds like the plane was a hit."

"He loved it. Asked if we could take it to Harper's tomorrow night."

"Is he staying there?"

"Yeah. Ethan wants him to sleepover. Harper's doing a cookout. Well. Harper says Keith is doing a cookout."

"How is she?"

"She got her cast off," I answer. "But she's in a boot for couple of weeks."

Julie nods. She's sitting on her bed again, but she's still dressed in a cute red top. Still has makeup on. Pretty, but I'd rather see her without makeup and curled up against her pillow ready to sleep.

"Did you go out tonight?"

"Yeah, Dani and I went to a bar. She got nachos with a side of heartburn."

"Did you?"

"No. I feel fine."

"I mean when you were pregnant. Did you have heartburn? Or morning sickness?"

Julie stares at me silently for a moment, and I hold my breath. Too soon to ask? Or maybe I don't have the right to ask at all?

"Yes and yes."

I nod. "Finding any hot guys on the beach?"

"None to write home about," she answers with a tiny smirk.

"Can I tell you I miss you?"

"I miss you, too, Truman."

"Dad?"

I turn my head when I hear Ryle at the door.

"What's up, Ryle?"

"Can I have pizza?"

"Now?"

I hear Julie snort on her end of the call.

"I'm hungry."

"How about a cookie and some milk?"

"The chocolate chip cookies Grandma made?"

"Yep."

"Okay."

"I'll be out in a minute."

I watch him zoom down the hall to the kitchen and look back at Julie, expecting a frown. Again, she surprises me with a big smile.

"Good job."

"Cookies are okay? Before bedtime?"

"Better than pizza," she says with a shrug.

"This kid." I raise my eyebrows. "Keeps you on your toes."

"You're not kidding." She covers a yawn and then grins and says sorry. "Like the time he asked me where puppies come from."

"He did? What'd you say?"

"The pet store." She shrugs again. "What else?"

"You wouldn't believe the conversation we had today."

"What?"

She looks tired. Besides, if I have the guts to get into this with her, if I tell her I want to marry her, it'll be when she's right here by my side. I'm not even going to mention the word over the phone.

"I'll tell you when you get home."

"That's not fair," she whines. "Now I'll be thinking about that the rest of my trip."

"I've thought about you every second you've been gone."

She squeezes her eyes closed and sends my heart to the floor again.

"Too much?" I ask quietly.

She shakes her head and finally opens her eyes again. "No."

"Julie?"

"Hmm?"

I hesitate. We've said we're not going to rush into things. But I've been dying to say these words for six years. Seven years, actually. It's been that long. And besides, if I'm going to bring up the conversation Ryle and I had today, if I'm going to bring it up in hopes that she'll say yes to getting married, I have to say it and the sooner, the better.

"I love you."

"Truman."

She squeezes her eyes closed again, and she makes this little noise, and I'm not sure if it was a laugh or a sob. I hold my breath and wait what feels like a million years before she opens her eyes again. Her lashes are wet with tears. I should've waited. I shouldn't have pushed it. She's going to run—

"I love you, too."

She ends the call before I can say more, and I sit on the edge of my bed. Stunned. Elated.

"Daaadd!"

I jump to my feet and toss the iPad on the bed. I think I might have a cookie and some milk with Ryle. I find him at the counter on his knees, waiting for me. He's wearing his Handy Manny pajamas, even though he deemed them too childish last night.

He watches me stick four cookies on a plate in the microwave.

"Why four?" he asks as I get the milk out.

"Two for you and two for me," I tell him.

"Mom doesn't zap them." He sounds worried. I glance at him and see him watching the microwave.

"We'll have to teach her to do that," I tell him. "Then they're gooey and warm like straight from the oven."

"Grandma gives them to me like that."

"Of course she does. Who do you think taught me to microwave them?"

I have no idea if my mom taught me that, but it seems possible.

Ryle grins.

"I wish Mom was here."

"Me too."

We're having fun, but by now, I'm sure Ryle is missing Julie. He's never been away from her for so long at a time.

"Is she having fun?"

"She told us she is, remember?"

"Is she tired?"

"I think so."

"Tired of being my mom?"

I freeze at the microwave and turn back to him. "Why would you say that, Ryle?"

He shrugs. "Maybe she's giving me to you now. So I can live with you."

Oh boy.

I take a deep breath, get the plate from the microwave, and put it on the counter by my little boy. All that talk today made him seem so much older, but right now, he's a sad, scared little boy who misses his mom, and doesn't know how to tell his dad how much.

"No." I shake my head. "Mom would never do that. She's tired right now because she and Dani were in the sun all day. Silly girls. You know Mom doesn't let you stay out in the sun, in a pool, all day, right?"

He nods, so I keep talking.

"So, she's had too much sun. And then they went out to eat, and she's tired. She just needs some sleep. Another day or two of girl time. And then she'll be home."

"'kay."

"Ryle, Mom misses you, too. You know that."

"I know."

He takes a drink and reaches for a cookie. "Are they still hot?"

I pick one up and take a small bite. "Kind of. Just blow on it."

We eat our cookies quietly, both of us lost in thought.

"So." I clear my throat. "Just so you know, you can spend the night here whenever you want."

"I can?"

"Yep." I nod and take a big drink. Ryle giggles when I put my cup down. "What?"

"You have a milk mustache."

I shrug. "I'll shave it off before we go to bed."

"Dad!" He snorts. "You don't shave milk mustaches."

"You don't?"

"No, you wash your face."

"Oh." I nod. "Okay."

Ryle licks his thumb and reaches over to smudge it over my upper lip.

"Did you just do the mom-thing to me?" I snatch his hand and pull him from his chair. He squeals when I tickle him.

"Mom does that all the time."

"Yep, it's a mom thing."

Still holding him, I stack our now empty cups and carry them and the plate to the sink.

"Let's go shave."

"No!" he laughs. "We brush our teeth now."

"Oh, right. Okay."

We brush side by side and then I follow him into the room I

was considering redecorating for him. Now I have other plans.

"What're we doing tomorrow?" he asks me when he lays down and I pull his sheet up and make a ridiculous deal out of tucking it under his chin.

"Going to Aunt Harper's."

"In the day," he says.

"Hmm. We could go drive the go-karts at Uncle Twain's."

"Can we?!"

"Sure." I nod. "But first. We have something very important to do."

"What?"

I sit on the edge of his bed. "We have to go shopping."

"No!" He rolls his head on his pillow. "I don't like shopping. Mom does that. It's boring."

"We're going shopping for Mom."

"What're we getting her?"

"You'll see." I ruffle his hair and lean over to kiss his forehead. "Goodnight, Ryle."

"Night, Daddy."

CHAPTER TWENTY-FIVE

Julie

Truman offered to drive Ryle home so I wouldn't have to stop and pick him up on the way from the airport. At first, I wanted to argue. I miss my little boy so much. All I want to do is pick him up and squeeze him. Drop a few thousand kisses all over his face. But now that I'm back in Basset and almost home, I'm glad I agreed.

Dani and I had a great time in Florida. Despite the heartburn and her bouts of morning sickness, she's not showing yet, and she's past that initial stage of having no energy. So we walked the beach and did some shopping, all the while talking and making plans. She and Eric are planning to turn their spare bedroom into a nursery, so we talked paint colors and stars on the ceiling or not. We tried to guess the sex of the baby, and we imagined her child in the future—at Ryle's age and older. We talked about Ryle, too. Dani loves that he played tee-ball this year. Even she's noticed how vocal he's become, and she's as relieved and happy about that as I am.

But now that I'm home, I feel like I need a vacation from my vacation. Seems like I say that anytime I go anywhere. I'll unpack and start laundry and maybe dinner, I decide as I glance at my watch. Ryle will be hungry.

Truman's car is parked in front of my house. Perfect. I'll get to see my boy and smother him with kisses and then get to work.

As happy as I am to see Ryle, though, he's not the reason for the hope burning a hole in my chest right now. I'm going to see Truman.

We've said it twice now. Friday and Saturday night on the phone.

Even more special to me? He said it first.

He loves me.

Between that, and Harper being the force that meddled us together, and Dani giving me her blessing and her hope, I feel like my feet don't hit the ground when I get out of the car to go inside. I float to the door, leaving my suitcase in the car. I'll get it later. Right now, I just want those arms around me.

Ryle's.

And Truman's.

The door opens as I reach for the handle. Ryle throws himself at me.

"Mom!"

"Ryle!" I scoop him up, ignoring the fact that he's getting heavy and too big for me to hold him. It makes me sad that he's growing up so fast, but for the first time ever, it crosses my mind that Truman and I could have another child.

"I missed you!" Ryle kisses my cheek, so I give him a noisy smooch on top of his head as I put him down.

"I missed you more!"

"Dad fixed you supper."

With Ryle's arms twined around my legs, I look over at Truman, who's standing by the stove. He's wearing an apron over his khaki shorts. I've never seen him in an apron; it's not a bad look.

"Hi." I feel shy suddenly, and I worry that the words we whispered over the phone weren't real.

"Hi." He raises his eyebrows hopefully. "Hope you're hungry."

I sniff garlic in the air and realize I am hungry.

"Dad fixed chicken parm."

"You did?" I look at Ryle and then back at Truman.

"And?" Truman prompts Ryle.

"I promised I would try the sauce."

"You did?" This time I look at Ryle with disbelief. He nods, but he looks miserable with his decision.

"But first!" Truman says. I glance at him. He's looking at Ryle.

"Yes!" Ryle does the celebratory fist bump and dashes out of the kitchen.

"Tell me everything," I say quietly. Truman unties the apron and tosses it on the counter. "Oh, I liked that look on you."

He grins as he comes close enough to slide his arms around my waist and pull me against him.

"You're here."

His whisper chases a chill down my back.

"I'm home."

I think I mean more than the fact that I'm standing in the house Ryle and I live in. But I'm so scared right now, I'm afraid to breathe, let alone say what I'm thinking.

"Julie." Truman kisses my cheek. "I love you."

Tears burn my eyes again, and suddenly, my arms are around him, and I'm holding tight, like I'm afraid he's going to disappear.

"I never stopped," he whispers. "Never."

"Hey!" Ryle yells and beelines for us when he comes back to the kitchen. I glance at him and see he's carrying his new remote control plane. Of course, he would want to show me that before he eats dinner. With spaghetti sauce. "Me, too."

Tears streak my face as he squeezes in between me and Truman.

"I want things to be different now," Truman whispers. There's so much we need to say to each other. Six years of things we held back, things we didn't share. But not here, not in front of Ryle.

"Me, too." I kiss Truman's cheek and thrill at the feel of his beard stubble on my skin. With a sniffle, I draw away from him and look at Ryle. "'kay. Show me your plane, pilot."

"Why are you crying?" he asks with a frown. He shoots a look of worry at Truman.

"Happy tears," I tell him.

"What are happy tears?"

"The way Grandma cries when she watches the wedding movie."

"Wedding movie?" I ask Truman.

"*The Princess Diaries*."

"Oh." I nod, but Ryle takes my hand and tugs me toward the door. "Okay. Let's go."

We go out to our little backyard, and the two of them wander a few feet away, whispering like they're conspiring. I have no idea what they're planning, but I love watching them together and wondering what they're up to.

"Ready?" Truman asks as he backs away.

"Yep." Ryle studies the remote in his hand, and then the little airplane slowly lifts from the ground. It's a bumpy ride, as the little toy flies higher.

"Doing great, buddy," Truman calls from my side. Ryle gets the plane a little higher, but he panics when it gets close to the big tree on the side of the yard. "It's okay. Just bring it in to land."

Ryle nods when Truman coaches him.

I admire the father of my son as he sticks his hands in his pockets and moseys out to stand by Ryle, and Ryle brings the plane down little by little. The landing is a bit rough, and I laugh softly, thinking it's actually pretty realistic. Ryle squats down over the plane like something's wrong.

"What happened?" I ask. Truman leans over Ryle, so I cross the yard to stand with them. "Did something break?"

"Nope." Ryle stands and picks the plane up to show me. Someone—my guess is Truman—painted our names on the side of the toy. Small gold letters spell out Truman, Jules, and Ryle.

"That's cool." I swallow down the lump in my throat and glance at Truman.

"Mom?" Ryle taps my arm. I love him, but I wish I could have a moment alone with Truman right now.

"What, Ryle?" I tear my gaze from Truman and see something on the wing of the plane. Some kind of gold plastic. "It did break. What is that?" I reach for the plane.

Truman takes the plane and pulls whatever I saw off the wing. He hands it to Ryle and then Ryle looks at me with a big, sloppy grin.

The same grin Truman wears when I look at him.

"Mom, will you marry Dad?"

Ryle holds up a gold ring. I stare at the ring, somewhat relieved it's not real. Because what if I said no? What would that do to Ryle? And what if I wanted to say yes, and the ring fell off the wing of the plane and got lost?

"If I eat sauce with my chicken parm, and Dad tells you you're beautiful every day?"

"Ryle." I laugh and sniffle again. What if this isn't real? What if this is something Ryle wanted to do? Maybe the second Ryle walks away, Truman might laugh and shake his head and say "kids. What're you gonna do?"

"What do you say, Jules?" Truman takes the ring from Ryle and lowers himself to one knee. "Will you marry me?"

I laugh when he slides the gaudy gold ring on my finger.

"Did you get this from a bubble gum machine?"

"Of course not." Truman rolls his eyes. "We went to a real toy store for this. And it was buy one get one half off, so there's a matching pair of clip-on earrings for you, too."

"Nice."

"Jules?" Truman grips my hand harder. Ryle stares at me with big, innocent eyes.

"Yes."

"We don't have to rush a wedding—"

"Dad, she said yes!" Ryle nudges Truman's shoulder.

"But I need you to know this is—"

"Truman." I lean forward and cup his face in my hands. "I said yes." I kiss him. A long, mushy kiss that makes Ryle groan out loud.

"Oh no. Not this."

I pull Truman to his feet, and he sweeps Ryle up and throws him over his shoulder as we trek back to the house.

"Oh yeah," Truman tells him. "You bet I get to kiss your mom now. All the time."

Ryle sighs like he's grossed out. "Do I have to eat the sauce?"

"You said you would try it," Truman reminds him.

Ryle looks to me for help when Truman puts him down once we're in the kitchen.

"If you told Daddy you would try it, I think you should try it."

"Great." He rolls his eyes. "Now you're ganging up on me."

I laugh as I sink down to a kitchen chair and pull Ryle into my lap.

"Where do you learn this stuff?" I mumble as I kiss the top of his head again.

"Dad says maybe you'll get me a baby brother."

Stunned at Ryle's comment, I glance at Truman to find him laughing behind his hands.

"Go wash up for dinner," Truman tells Ryle. We watch our son run from the room and then look at each other. "He asked for one. I didn't volunteer the offer."

"Do you want more kids?" I ask him when he leans over me.

"I do," he says with a nod, "but you know what I want first?"

"What?"

"I want to know everything you felt and did when you were pregnant with him."

"Truman." I wrap my fingers around the back of his neck and press my lips to his.

"Tell me everything, Jules."

Thank you for reading Truman & Julie's story. Please consider leaving a review on Amazon, Goodreads, or other bookish websites.

Turn the page to read a bonus chapter of Rings on Wings

BONUS CHAPTER

Julie's on the dance floor. She's out there with the girls, and she keeps signaling for me to join them. I want to. I like to dance, and I love any reason, any excuse, to get close to her. But for just this moment, I don't move. I'm happy to stand here and watch the love of my life having fun with the other important girls in my life.

You'd never know Harper was in a car accident last summer if you hadn't seen her in the cast, plunking around on crutches. She's dancing her heart out—even the weird dances my niece is into these days. Interesting how The Floss and The Wobble look pretty ridiculous until I watch Julie do the dance steps. Then they look kind of cute. Kind of sexy.

Keith joins me at the table. He's got a little grin on his face. Odds are, he's thinking the same thing about Harper, but since she's my sister, I don't ask. The thing is, though, she looks happy. Harper, Mom, Mabry, Julie—they're having the time of their lives right now, and all I want is to stand here and soak it all up.

"She's not sorry, you know."

I glance at Keith and shrug. Harper's not sorry for meddling in my personal life. I know that. And she'd do it again tomorrow if she thought it was necessary. Maybe I should be wary of that; there might be a time when her meddling is more of a problem, but how can I be angry right now? Besides, if I thought Keith and Harper were having problems, I think I'd have a hard time keeping my mouth shut.

The song changes to something by Bruno Mars, and I roll my eyes at the collective whoops and hollers on the dance floor.

"I like to watch her move," Keith says quietly.

"Me, too." I nod, though I know he's talking about Harper, and I'm talking about Julie.

Julie catches my eye again and waves me out. I hold up a hand as if to ask for a minute. And then my dad joins the girls, and it looks like he's singing along with the lyrics. I had no idea my dad was familiar with a current beat, let alone "Uptown Funk" lyrics.

My parents met in this skating rink. They tell the story often. Dad would come in and watch Mom skate, and he finally had to give it a shot to catch her eye. When I was younger, their love story made me roll my eyes. When I got older and found myself in love with Julie, it was easier to listen to. When Jules and I split, my parents' love story made me feel like there was something wrong with me.

After all, it was my fault that Jules and I split up.

Now, though, Julie and I are together, and I'm happy. This is my new life, and I never want it to change. As I look around the rink, the flash of neon lights illuminating my family members, and the one thing in common the way everyone is smiling, I know I owe it all to my parents. They fell in love, and they raised us in that loving home and showed us how to do it. Maybe it took me a bit to figure that out, but better late than never.

Twain appears in the corner of my eye. He's talking to someone he went to school with. My brother lives in denim and flannel, so the sight of him in the tux and bow tie this morning was a shock. But his smile was all Twain, and his happiness was contagious, and I'm immature enough to admit that his little nervous streak was fun to see.

He's holding a champagne flute. That's new. He's usually a longneck bottle guy. I look from him to his bride, out there on the floor with my bride-to-be. Her dress is simple but elegant, and it's perfect for her. And for Twain. I'm not sure two people were ever more right for each other.

Except maybe Jules and me.

Mabry's holding her flute, too, but it doesn't look so out of place in her hand. Her sister joins the group, and the song changes again. This time it's a fifties song. I don't know the DJ tonight, but he or she has my total approval. Wedding receptions are for dancing, and the skating rink has been packed most of the night. Twain hasn't even batted an eye at the thought of having the floor redone when the night is over. Then again, he and Mabry are flying out for the Amalfi Coast tomorrow, so I'm sure the skating rink, Wolverine Park—his little slice of the Woolff Empire, and all of us are the last thing on his mind.

Suddenly, Ryle slides his leg over mine, and his boney little butt cuts my thigh. My son has grown a foot taller in the last several months. He's tall and lanky, a little bit like his Uncle Twain. Since my brother is a pretty good guy, I'm okay with that, and I'm hoping he grows up with more of Twain's qualities.

"Where ya been?" I ask Ryle. He hooks a long, skinny finger in the top of plastic soda cup and lifts it to his mouth. He drinks, lifting a finger to say just a second. He's out of breath when he puts the cup down and looks at me. I suppose I had soda mustaches as a kid, but I've never seen one before watching my son dive into a cup and gulp the liquid down.

"With Ethan," he answers. His breath smells like cola. Eyes wide, he rests his hand on my chest. The reception has been going on for a couple of hours now. I've taken my suit coat off, rolled my sleeves up, and yanked the tie from my collar. Still hot, but it's bearable.

"Havin' fun?"

He nods, but he seems distracted.

"What's wrong?" I ask him.

"You said you'd get me a baby brother."

This again. I suck in a deep breath and start to answer him, but Ryle cuts me off.

"How come you said you would, and it's Aunt Harper who's pregnant?"

"What?"

I'm glad I'm sitting down. I glance over the table to my brother-in-law, but he's not paying attention to us.

"Ethan said Aunt Harper's pregnant."

"And how does Ethan know that?" I tip my head, ready to shrug the big reveal off and tell Ryle it's best not to talk about grown up things.

"Because Aunt Harper and Uncle Keith told him and Hattie and Craig."

Hmm.

I clamp my mouth shut before a sharp laugh can slip out.

"I wanted a baby," Ryle mumbles.

"Buddy." I lean forward and sling my arm around Ryle's shoulders. "Mom and I want that, too."

"Then just get one."

"Not that easy."

"Well, how do you do it?" Ryle asks me. "Ethan says you have to kiss a lot. Craig said you have to—"

"The first thing Mom and I have to do is get married."

Ryle sighs. "You had me. And you weren't."

I look at the dance floor, wishing Julie was on her way over to save me. Instead, she and Harper are crooning to "Stars on 45" and dancing in perfect rhythm.

"You're right." I nod. "But this time, we want to be married first. And we'll all live in the same house, and then maybe, we'll have a baby."

"Will I be in your wedding?" he asks me.

I actually slump back in my chair I'm so relieved he's moved on from the baby subject.

"Yep."

"Like Bryson was in Uncle Twain's?"

Mabry's nephew, Bryson, was their ring-bearer. Ethan will be our ring-bearer. The girls hashed all of those details out so there would be no hurt feelings.

"No."

"No?" Ryle draws back with a deep frown on his face. "Why not?"

"Because you're my son," I say simply, "And I need you to be my best man."

"What does that mean?"

"It means you have one of the most important jobs at me and Mom's wedding."

Ryle thinks that over.

"What do I have to do?"

"You gotta stand right by me at the front of the church. And you have to make sure I'm not nervous."

"Like you did for Uncle Twain."

"Like I did for Uncle Twain," I agree.

Ryle suddenly looks a foot taller.

"Think you can do that?" I ask.

"Yeah," he answers with an enthusiastic nod.

"Perfect." I stand and ease him from my lap. My thigh feels dead where his bones dug in.

"Where are you going?"

"To dance with your mom."

He considers that for a moment, and I think he might come with me. But then he darts off the other way, most likely in search of Ethan and Bryson. The girls part their little circle when I join them, and just in time, the music changes, and Julie steps into my arms as the opening notes of "Still the One" play.

"You sure you don't want to elope?" I ask her.

She laughs softly and rests her hand on my chest. Knowing I'm joking, she doesn't even bother answering me. Mabry and Harper catcall my parents when Dad dips Mom, and Jules and I laugh together. Because someday that will be us, and we'll still be together.

"Not a chance, Truman Woolff," she finally says and pats my chest. I take her hand in mine, fingers grazing over the diamond solitaire I gave her to replace the gawdy plastic ring Ryle and I proposed with.

She carries that one with her everywhere in her purse.

PLUS ONE

Chapter 1

Cait

The last time I flew across the country to California I was with my sister and her family. We were heading to Disneyland for my niece's birthday, because turning five is apparently a big deal nowadays. I think I got a new doll and my sister's hand-me-down bike for my fifth birthday, but whatever. The whole family enjoyed Stella's birthday, so there's that, I guess.

Anyway, back to the fact that I'm stuck in Row 17, on Southwest Flight 472, bound for wine country. Sounds perfect, right? I mean, given a choice, I'd rather be in like, *Row 6*, but still—wine country! If your destination is wine country, that makes up for any inconveniences on your flight, right?

Well, no. Not really.

The only thing worse than my current situation is that I could be sitting in the middle seat, stuck between my best friend Teagan and her guy, Derrick—lovey-dovey newlyweds—instead of in the window seat on the flight to my other bestie's destination wedding in wine country.

Well, I mean, I guess I could be flying to, like, Detroit for a destination wedding. Or anything, really, other than wine country.

I like my wine. Brynna, Teagan, and I all like our wine. Sure, we started our drinking career many years ago— maybe when we were underage, but I won't confirm that. Anyway, we started our careers with the cheap beer pretty much every high school—strike that—every young person starts with. Because first of all, it's cheap, and when you need to spend your money on jeans and shoes and cute tops, who has cash leftover for beer? Second? Well, none of us liked the taste of beer back then, so why would we want to pass up a new pair of gladiator sandals or Miss Me bootcuts for something we didn't even like?

From beer, we tiptoed into whiskey, but let me tell you, that stuff was way worse than beer. Then again, maybe some of that reflects on our mixologists. Show me a high school kid— I mean, a younger, inexperienced drinker—who can make a mean Old Fashioned, and I'm calling bullshit. We all took our turns doing the mixing, and yeah, we were all equally bad. Maybe part of that was because when you're young, the sole purpose of drinking is to get blitzed and be stupid, right? Not to enjoy the *taste* of something.

We didn't venture into wine until we were in our early twenties, definitely of age. And those first forays into the wine world were box wines and the two buck chuck stuff that tasted either like Kool-Aid or cough medicine. I'll never forget the first time Teagan killed a bottle of that stuff on her own. Teag loves to talk, and when you add alcohol, you seriously can't get her to stop talking. Pretty sure she recited the entire preamble to the Constitution that night. But she did it with a bunch of corny, badly done accents.

Teagan taps my arm now. I pause the music on my phone and take an ear bud out as I turn to her.

"You brought the stuff, right?"

"Yep."

She nods. "But. I mean. You brought everything. Right?"

"Got it," I promise her. By stuff, she's referring to the few gag gifts and bachelorette sorts of things she and I got for Brynna, our friend who would be a beautiful bride in just four days.

"Okay." She smiles and relaxes back into her seat.

The three of us met in first grade. Teagan was the chatterbox, the most outgoing of all of us, and the one who had to write *I will not talk in class* at least five times a year starting in fourth grade. In first grade, she had a bowl haircut, and her smile was missing a front tooth. Took forever for that tooth to grow in because it didn't come out naturally. She and her older brother—River's a year older than we are—were wrestling in their living room, and River knocked Teagan face first into the coffee table. Knocked her tooth out. She's gorgeous now with short, spiky dark hair and a friendly smile, but if you know what you're looking for, you can see that her tooth didn't grow in as perfectly as the rest of them.

"But." She leans forward again and curls her fingers around my wrist. I eye her thick white gold wedding band and lift my eyes to hers. "Did you remember the body paint?"

"Teag." I tip my head at her. "It's all under control."

She studies my face to make sure she can trust me. Because normally, I am the forgetful one. I can make a long list of things to pack for a trip, and you better believe, I'm still going to forget something. Every. Time.

Not this time, though. I made sure to pack every last fun little gift we got for Brynna: from the slinky, sexy stuff to the kinky, funny stuff, to the actual real gifts we had picked out for our friend. I even have a gorgeous wine-colored gift bag that says *Bride to Be* in silver sparkles. The whole lot of it is the first thing I packed for the trip.

"'Kay." She smiles. Drags her front teeth—the right one is just a tiny bit shorter than the other one—over her lip. And then she snorts this cute little giggle that makes Brynna nuts. "She's gonna die."

Die of embarrassment, she means.

"Well, either that, or she'll kill us." I shrug.

Teagan closes her eyes, that smile still on her lips. I look past her to Derrick, who has his nose stuck in a Dean Koontz book. Like always. Not that I don't love a good Dean Koontz book, too. Derrick must feel my eye roll—about their joined hands resting on Teag's leg, not because of the book— because he takes a quick peek at me.

Don't get me wrong. Love the guy. He's the perfect match for Teagan. He's the calm to her crazy. The quiet to her loud. The thought to her impulsiveness. They started dating when we were seniors in college. Brynna and I wondered if maybe they were shooting for a longest dating relationship before they got married last year.

So, yeah, okay. Boxed wine.

Well, I mean, thank God we graduated from that stuff. Some of us have experimented and found we actually like craft beers, and by some of us I mean Teagan and me. Give Brynna any kind of beer, and she'll just turn her nose up and go in search of good wine. Teag and I have taken to some mixed drinks, too, and an occasional shot of bourbon or whiskey.

But the three of us definitely love our wine.

Now that we're grownups, we've traded in the two buck chuck stuff for real-deal California wines. Brynna's aunt and uncle moved to wine country when we were first learning the ropes of drinking and sucking on pennies to get the alcohol off our breath so we could hide that we were breaking parental rules and real laws. The three of us have always been sort of family fluid, so on any given weekend, one of our houses could have all three of us there, leaving the other two families without their daughters.

Well, in my case, without their youngest daughter.

Don't take it the wrong way, but through the years, we were so close, that our parents were interchangeable. I was just as used to waking up in Brynna or Teagan's room as mine. My mom did their laundry. Teag's mom helped Brynna and me with our science homework. Brynna's parents took us along on several family vacations. To the beach. To amusement parks.

And finally, to wine country. We were eighteen the first time we went. It was for Brynna's high school graduation, and even though we couldn't legally drink at the wineries, Brynna's aunt and uncle had quite a personal wine collection, and we were allowed to taste the good stuff under their watchful adult eyes.

And we might have pilfered a bottle or two through the years when we visited. Brynna's Uncle Tom marked the value on the bottom of each bottle with a silver pen. We were careful not to take anything we thought was too expensive. And we were careful tiptoeing down the steps of their house and sneaking out to the patio to sip wine and rehash old times and share our hopes and dreams.

Brynna was the most sentimental of the three of us. When we were twelve, she was in love with Henry Mason. I mean, it was almost comical the way her eyes bugged out of her head when he walked by us in the halls at school. She wrote his name on the inside of all of her notebooks in eighth grade. Drew hearts with his initials in them. Henry was clueless. He was kind of a dumb jock, though. Taller than most of the boys, and even then, he was almost twice as wide as most of them. Not fat wide, but football player wide.

Brynna loved a lot of guys through the years. Some of them loved her back. And one of them—Theo Garvey—really loved her back. They dated from the beginning of sophomore year until they went away for college. Theo found someone else before college freshmen orientation was over. He was a nice guy, but girl code clearly states that you never say that around the bestie that he dumped. So. Theo became the jerk that we didn't name. Brynna was broken-hearted. It took her a long time to date again.

Even then, she wanted us to find our guys. Or, as she started saying when we were older, our person. She's always been a flowery, sweet, feminine girl, and she loves romance, and she's always happy. She sees the good in everyone, and she wants happiness for everyone, so she tends to be a bit heavy-handed with dating advice and arranging for meet cutes for all of her friends.

Well, Teag doesn't have to deal with that anymore, right? We all thought Brynna would be the first down the aisle, but Teagan shocked us and did the *I dos* and so now, it's just me, fortunate enough to get all of my best friends' attention and set ups.

Really. It's just me.

Like, at midnight last night, my boyfriend Ryan was supposed to hop a different flight this morning—he's been in Boston the past few days—to meet me in Sonoma for the wedding. And this morning, just before Derrick beeped the horn of their Honda Passport to let me know he and Teagan were waiting in the drive to head for the airport, Ryan called and let me know he couldn't make it.

Yep.

Just like that.

Hey, Cait, listen, I'm sorry. But I can't make the wedding. Give Brynn and Adam my best.

Click here to download Plus One:

ALSO BY TRACY BROEMMER

Loved You More, Lorelei Bluffs, Book 8

A Lorelei Ending, Lorelei Bluffs, Book 9

I Do, Lorelei Bluffs, Book 10

Truth Is, The Williams Legacy, Book 1

Other People's Ugly, The Williams Legacy, Book 2

Omissions, The Williams Legacy, Book 3

Contemporary Romance Novels:

Destiny's Calling: Your Future Is Waiting

Wedding Day Shenanigans

Holiday Fling

The Kiss Off

Something Like Love

Plus One

Hold Onto the Stars, Book #5 in Blue Collar Romance series

The Jane Thing, Book #2 in Meet Cute Book Club series

Shameless Santa, Book #7 in Welcome to Kissing Springs series

Sunshine & Soulmates, Welcome to Kissing Springs, Sunshine Season

Bourbon & Bedposts, Book #7 in Welcome to Kissing Springs, Bourbon Season

Doctor Divine, Doctors of Eastport General, Season 2

Beach Daze, Flamingo Island

Moonlight in Montreal, The Vagabond Series

Christmas and Other Inconveniences, Betting on Christmas Collection

Eggnog in Amesbury, Christmas in Amesbury Series (Sweet Romance)

A December Wish, Wishing for Love Series (Sweet Romance)

A Naughty Lesson

Love, Nashville, The Mississippi Queen Trilogy, Book 1

Forever, Duncan, The Mississippi Queen Trilogy, Book 2

Always, Jess, The Mississippi Queen Trilogy, Book 3

Gettin' Hitched, The H Books, Book 1

Hookin' Up, The H Books, Book 2

Holdin' On, The H Books, Book 2.5

Intoxicate Me, 515 Whiskey, Book .5

Taste Me, 515 Whiskey, Book 1

Scrooge Me, 515 Whiskey, Bonus Short Story in Let's Get Naughty V 3

Contemporary Romance Novellas:

Indian Summer

Dear Jaclyn Perris

French Stuff

Holdin' On (The H Books)

End in Flames

Mistletoe Mishaps

Toasted: A New Year's Eve Novella

Endless Summer (Timberton Hounds)

Homeless Holiday (Timberton Hounds)

Restless Hearts (Timberton Hounds)

Timberton Hounds Novellas Boxset

Boone's Girl

Intoxicate Me (515 Whiskey)

Seducing You (Welcome to Kissing Springs and Lockland Distilling: Keys to Love)

Kissing You (Welcome to Kissing Springs and Lockland Distilling: Keys to Love)

Swipe for Fangs

Swipe for Ghouls

Feels on Wheels (Love in Motion Duet, Book 1) (Sweet Romance)

Rings on Wings (Love in Motion Duet, Book 2) (Sweet Romance)

Love in Motion Boxset

Other Novellas:

The Devy Man, A Horror Novella

Today, Again (Sweet Love Story)

Women's Fiction Short Stories:

India Falls

Luther's Cross: 87,600

The Candy Cane Tree of Willow Lane

Delays

Same Time Next Year

Contemporary Romance Short Stories:

Perfect Pictures, The Wine Tasting Series, Traminette (Sweet)

Coming Home, The Wine Tasting Series, Edelweiss (Sweet)

Save Me Every Dance, The Wine Tasting Series, Rosé (Sweet)

Marry Me, The Wine Tasting Series, Shiraz (Sweet)

Birthday Wishes, The Wine Tasting Series, Muscat (Sweet)

Dad Jeans, The Wine Tasting Series, Vignoles (Sweet)

The Wine Tasting Series Boxset (Sweet)

Peppermint Lane

Priceless Memory (Timberton Hounds)

Truly Dante, A Mississippi Queen Trilogy Short Story

Strawberry Wine

Love Letter

Leaving You, A Lockland Distilling: Keys to Love Short Story

Sambuca Santa

Deadman's Hollow

ABOUT THE AUTHOR

Tracy Broemmer is the author of several contemporary romance novels including the 515 Whiskey Series, the Welcome to Kissing Springs: Bourbon Fever Collection, and the Mississippi Queen Trilogy. Tracy also writes women's fiction and is the author of the Williams Legacy series as well as several stand-alone titles.

Tracy's books have been called gripping, emotional, and timely, and readers describe her characters as real and relatable.

Tracy lives in Midwestern Illinois with her husband of 31 years. Visit her on the web and sign up for her newsletter at www.broemmerbooks.com